Our Lady
of Everything

Our Lady
of Everything

SUSAN FINLAY

First published in Great Britain in 2019 by Serpent's Tail,
an imprint of PROFILE BOOKS LTD
3 Holford Yard
Bevin Way
London
WC1X 9HD
www.serpentstail.com

10 9 8 7 6 5 4 3 2 1

Typset in 10.75/13.5pt Freight Text by Nicky Barneby
Designed by Nicky Barneby @ Barneby Ltd
Printed and bound in Great Britain by Clays Ltd, Elcograf S.p.A.

A CIP record for this book can be obtained from the British Library

ISBN: 978 1 78816 119 0
eISBN: 978 1 78283 476 2

For Jane and Tess

'There is no purpose or grand cosmic scheme to life beyond what we choose to impose or believe. To some this is cynicism. For the Chaos Magician, it is a breath of dizzying freedom.'

– Phil Hine, *Condensed Chaos: An Introduction to Chaos Magic*

The Unequal Opportunities Rite: A Basic Banishing Ritual

LIKE EVERY BANISHING RITUAL, THE Unequal Opportunities Rite has two main aims, namely to clear the mind of mundane influences and to clear the surrounding atmosphere of other psychic debris, which, in this case, has built up through the continual misuse of categories as experienced via job applications, so-called academic research and various other schemes monitored by the government.

The Unequal Opportunities Rite entails the visualisation of coloured light within specific areas of the body. These areas correspond with the sections on the equal opportunities monitoring forms used by some institutions but not others, on account of the fact that most but not all institutions use very slightly different procedures. The Rite is designed to create psychic arcs, and thus to facilitate greater psychosomatic control over who and what the subject may, or may not, wish to be perceived as. It can be performed either by itself, or as a precursor to more elaborate magik.

RITE:
1. Stand with shoulders hunched and head lowered.
2. Inhale fully. Exhale slowly, and then mutter the words 'My ethnic origin is Asian, Black, White, Mixed, Other (Please Specify)' while visualising a red arc of light around the head.

3. Inhale fully. Exhale slowly, and then mutter the words 'My national identity is English, Welsh, Scottish, Northern Irish, British, Other (Please Specify)' while visualising a yellow arc of light around the throat.
4. Inhale fully. Exhale slowly, and then mutter the words 'My gender is Male, Female, Other (Please Specify), Prefer not to Say' while visualising a pink arc of light around the heart and lungs.
5. Inhale fully. Exhale slowly, and then mutter the words 'My age range is 16–24, 25–34, 35–44, 45–54, 55–64, 65+' while visualising a green arc of light around the stomach.
6. Inhale fully. Exhale slowly, and then mutter the words 'My religion or belief is No Religion, Buddhist, Christian, Hindu, Jewish, Muslim, Sikh, Other (Please Specify), Prefer not to Say' while visualising a purple arc of light around the genital/anal area.
7. Repeat steps six, five, four, three and two, working back from the genital/anal area towards the head.
8. Inhale fully. Exhale slowly, re-muttering each of the previous statements, while drawing an orange and then a blue arc with the left arm, each of which is also visualised strongly.
9. Make a quarter turn to the left and repeat step eight, and then continue to turn and draw the remaining coloured arcs with statements and visualisations until returning to the starting position.
10. Repeat steps two to seven inclusive, and then stand up straight, raise your head, point and shout out: 'Look! A rainbow!'

Margaret

MARGARET O'SHEA TEETERED ON THE edge of a large, elaborately patterned settee, designed according to a fantasy of luxury but constructed according to the reality of cheap materials. The settee, like the two, similarly recherché armchairs that accompanied it, either sucked the sitter into the spongy crack at the back, or else forced them to perch upon its periphery, while a selection of gilt-edged plates – part of a wall-mounted series – formed halos around their heads.

There was a calendar opposite, and on the middle of the mantelpiece beneath, a blue statuette of a woman. The bottom half of the calendar stated that it was August 2004, while the top half depicted roses. Whereas the ergonomics of the settee and the position of the plates transformed the living room's inhabitants into shipwrecked saints washed up in a drift of soft furnishings and then appealing to a ceramic heaven, the statuette and the calendar created a shrine, reminiscent of those from Margaret's childhood in a village just west of Belfast.

> Refuge in grief, star of the sea,
> Pray for the mourner, pray for me.

Margaret looked at the calendar and the statuette, and the words of a hymn flickered into her mind so that, for one brief

3

moment, she wondered if she was about to start singing. Only the noise from the clock, which kept on ticking, stopped her from doing so. Instead she pressed her lips together so that the words, like the tears, stayed in. Eleven ten, eleven eleven, eleven twelve – she heard the seconds and then the minutes jerk by. Eleven thirteen, eleven fourteen – and finally the telephone began to ring. Margaret made a grab for it, and then pressed it, desperately, against her ear, while the Holy Virgin (who was also the Holy Mother, who was also Our Lady of Sorrows, Grace, Light, Mercy, etc.) looked on – serene, or maybe just not moving.

'Nana?' said a man's voice, or more specifically 'na-narh', the vowels both flattened and lengthened in the standard East Midlands way, 'Nana it's me, it's Eoin.'

Margaret frowned, tapped the speaking end and then put the listening end back against her ear, but all she could hear was static. It was the same sound that her hearing aid made, which was the same reason that she didn't always wear it.

'Hello, Nottingham 9231426. This is Margaret O'Shea speaking.'

'Nana it's—'

'Eoin? Is that you?'

'Aye Nana. It's me. It's Eoin.'

'Eoin? Can you hear me? It's your Nana here ...'

And so it continued, as Margaret in Nottingham (or England, or the depths of the sea) and Eoin in Basra (or Iraq, or the heat of the desert) listened to each other repeat their own names and the names of each other into the crackling telephone receiver, each affirming and confirming the well-worn legacy of their displacement. Suddenly, however, the crackling stopped, so that Eoin became loud and harsh, and almost interrogative.

'And I mean to say, are you looking after yourself?'

Margaret made the breathy whistling sound that she used in place of laughter and then looked back at the statuette, and behind it the bottom half of the calendar, where eighteen crosses told her that Eoin had been away for eighteen days.

'I've had a novena for you.'

'Sorry Nana, what was that?'

'I've said the rosary for you, every day, for nine days.'

'But I've been away for—'

'I've had two.'

Margaret had had two novenas, which meant that she had said the rosary every day for eighteen days, and she would have eighteen novenas, which meant that she would say the rosary every day for each of the remaining 162 that Eoin wasn't here – although the thought that she was now praying for the life of an English soldier seemed more than a little crazy. Whenever she thought of English soldiers she thought of Bernadette Moran's boy running through her house and then out the back with two men in khakis pounding after him, back in her old home, in Ireland; and then, just like the old days, she pressed her lips together so that what mustn't get out stayed in . . .

'I've asked Kathy to stop by,' said Eoin.

'Ah come on. She'll have better things to do I'm sure.'

'Than visiting you Nana? Now that I find hard to believe.'

Margaret whistled again and this time Eoin joined in with her, letting out the same low rumbling that, ever since he was a child, had signified anxiety as much as anything else. As long as the laughter lasted, she could remember the nervous little boy that he used to be, and in many ways still was, rather than the man with the squaddie's thousand-yard stare in the passing out picture she'd immediately placed face-down in a drawer. She could remember how he had always gripped her hand on the journey to school, but then dropped it as soon as the gates came into view, trying to make it seem as if he were arriving there alone. Once, on their way home, they had found a fallen nest with a baby bird in it, and he had insisted that they take it back with them and look after it until it was well. She had filled a sherry glass with milk and showed him how to feed the bird from it, as well as how to make a cake for it out of leftover fat and seeds, all of which he had then done with slow, meticulous concentration. She could remember how much he had loved *The Really Wild Show*, and how he collected the stickers associated with it and told her that when he grew up he was going to be a vet and look after animals too –

and she had wished it were possible, but knew that it wasn't, because people like them were still people like them ... The laughter stopped. Eoin paused, raised his voice and said, 'But how are you Nana? How's St Flannan's?'

'Well last week another Rwandan family started coming. And now also a woman from Malawi.'

'Malawi?'

'Yes. Her name is Blessings.' Margaret tapped the receiver, and then rubbed her knees, which ached. 'But what about the weather? Is it nice out there? Is it hot?'

'Aye Nana it is. Very. Although it can get cold at night.'

'Then you need sunscreen and a warm jacket. Have you got sunscreen and a warm jacket Eoin? Have you—'

'Aye Nana. I've got all those things and more. Even the dogs have coats.'

'You have dogs?'

Eoin laughed again.

'A few army dogs, yes.'

Margaret, who throughout their conversation had been slowly sucked back into the cushions, now wriggled forwards, and then, as soon as she reached the edges of the settee, planted both her feet, very firmly, on the ground. Over the past eighteen days she had tried, many times, to picture the country that Eoin had gone to because of a war, bits and pieces of which she had seen played back on the television, just as she had tried to picture Rwanda, the country that the new black families had come from, or even Malawi, the country that Blessings had left; and although lions and tigers had featured heavily in her imaginings, something as ordinary as a dog had never occurred to her. Now that it did, however, she was comforted – Eoin had always wanted a puppy.

'I'm sorry that I never let you have a puppy.'

But the crackling rose again, forcing Margaret to resume her tapping and Eoin his shouting until the sounds of their disconnect and their failure to overcome it too soon became exhausting.

'I'll say goodbye then Nana!' shouted Eoin.

'Oh? Well goodbye then. God bless.'

There was a click, and the crackling stopped. Slowly Margaret put down the receiver, and then, without any warning, threw the telephone onto the floor. And then she sat in what would have been silence except that the clock just wouldn't stop ticking.

Katarzyna

KATARZYNA KWIATKOWSKA PRESSED THE DOORBELL and waited. Then she pressed it again. And again. And then she started to wonder if the thing that caused Margaret's selective deafness was the same thing that sometimes made her lose her balance, and whether or not this, together with what she knew of her knees, meant that Margaret might have fallen now.

Katarzyna pressed the bell one last time, and as she did so it occurred to her that she couldn't hear anything coming out of it. She realised that it must have broken, and that Margaret, not wanting to be any bother, which was in itself a bother, would be suffering, quite literally, in silence – all of which left her with little other option than to bang loudly, and slightly irritably, on the door. Then she took off her baseball cap and bent down so that her mouth was level with the letterbox, pushed it open and shouted, 'Margaret are you there?'

'Margaret are you there!' came a high, sarcastic voice from behind her.

Katarzyna turned round and saw that the group of boys by the bus stop were laughing. She stuck two fingers up at them and then bent down again.

'It's Kathy—'

'It's Kathy!'

'And I've come to—'

'And I've come to!'

'Kathy is that you?' came Margaret's voice from inside the house.

'Aye Margaret it's me.'

'Aye Margaret it's me!'

Katarzyna picked up a pebble and threw it at one of the boys, who only just dodged it, and then turned back around and listened to the sound of Margaret's shuffling as it made its way towards her. She could hear the key moving inside first the bottom lock and then the top one, and then the faint but clunky sound of a heavy bolt being drawn back, and finally Margaret herself appeared.

'Now you'll have a cup of tea won't you Kathy? I've just put the kettle on.'

'Sure, I mean yeah, yeah that'd be great.'

Katarzyna bent down again and kissed her, and then shut the door behind them both and followed Margaret inside. She perched on one of the armchairs while Margaret shuffled off into the kitchen, and stared at the calendar, the crosses on which made her think of prison. She had been with Eoin since her eighteenth birthday party at Black Orchid, a tacky nightclub which she had hated, but which all her friends, at that time, had loved. One of Eoin's friends had asked one of her friends if Eoin could buy her a celebratory drink, while he lingered a few paces behind her at the bar – so handsome, but also nervous, as if he'd somehow borrowed his good looks from someone else. She had been charmed to think that he might feel as lost as she did in that screechy, sparkly place, and when he had finally asked for her number at the end of the night she had surprised herself not only by writing down a real one, but also by hoping, with quiet desperation, that he would actually call it. Afterwards, her friends had been horrified not only by the pub to which he'd taken her for a drink but also that she'd agreed to go, because it was the kind of pub that only old men drank in, and it smelled of sweat and beer – yet she had been so pleased to go to somewhere unpretentious, where they could hide as well as talk.

9

And then, gradually, they revealed themselves to each other. Like her, Eoin had left school early and like her he had always read in secret, although it was factual books about animals and plants, rather than novels, that he preferred. Like her, he had a shitty job but dreamed of other, better, things, and like her he didn't yet know what those things were. Over time, her so-called friends had stopped being her friends altogether, and her parents, like his Nana, had slipped into the background of their lives until it was just the two of them against the world ... And yet, although she knew that she would never love anyone the same way she still loved Eoin now, she also knew that what they had been, had been of the moment, and thus she still struggled to picture anything, least of all herself, as far ahead as six months' time. She took a deep breath and, allowing these two contradictory things to churn inside her, raised her voice and shouted, 'If the doorbell's broken then I can get my dad to fix it!'

'Ah come on now, he's got better things to do I'm sure.'

Katarzyna craned her neck towards the kitchen door, and as she did so her gaze fell upon the telephone that appeared to have been wrenched from its socket.

'And the phone too if needs be!'

'You're too kind Kathy. Too kind. But I'm not on my last legs yet.'

'No, no of course not. I only meant that he's often down here with work.'

'Well perhaps. But only if he was passing.'

'Oh he's always passing, and always stopping too' – she smiled as Margaret shuffled back in with the tea things – 'especially if there's biscuits!'

Margaret whistled breathily and then held out a plate of custard creams, one of which Katarzyna dutifully placed on the side of her saucer.

'So Eoin tells me that you're living in Forest Fields now?' said Margaret.

'Yeah, yeah I have been for a few months.'

'But couldn't you afford somewhere nice?' And on the word

'nice' Margaret sighed. 'Like West Bridgford say? I mean you went to a good school there didn't you?' And on 'good' she sighed again. 'If only my own daughter, God rest her soul, had had her wits about her . . .'

Katarzyna nodded at the carpet and then broke her custard cream in half, and then in half again. She knew that 'nice' meant away from the drugs and prostitutes that Forest Fields had always had a reputation for; and that 'good' meant Catholic, although the constant snobberies that she had been forced to endure for five years, by virtue of her baptismal certificate, at English Martyrs secondary school, had felt like anything but a 'good' experience to her. Likewise, she understood that Margaret's unfinished sentence was because she only wanted to imply what she thought, namely that if Eoin's mother had had her wits about her, then she'd have seen to it that he also went to English Martyrs, and got some GCSEs, meaning options, other than the army . . . She put down her custard cream, smiled a nice, good smile and said, 'Well I only work on classified ads. It doesn't really pay that much and, you know, I want to save what I can for the wedding.'

'But you'll finish your course soon, at New College. And then you'll be a proper journalist.'

'Yes, maybe.'

'No, definitely.'

Katarzyna tried to smile again but then discovered that she couldn't. She knew that if she had really wanted to be a proper journalist, that if she too had had her wits about her, then she should have attempted to fulfil the 'considerable potential' that every single one of her teachers wrote about on every single one of her school reports. Her ability to absorb and then retain any piece of information, and then piece it together with others, under exam conditions, and with not inconsiderable flair, hadn't gone unnoticed, just as her foreignness, and working-classness – which had generally been viewed as a one-and-the-same-type-of-chavvinesss – hadn't either. The other girls went to English Martyrs because they lived in the area, and their parents, who were usually doctors, or lawyers, or teachers, knew that Catholic

11

schools got good results, unlike hers, who had made her go because God was always watching. None of the other girls had the
local accent that she did, and all of them wore clothes on wear-
your-own-clothes day that she could never afford. From the very
beginning she had been an anomaly, and her cleverness, which
she soon learned to hide, had only made it worse. By the time
she had finished her GCSEs the opportunity to escape the snide
remarks about her chavvy accent and her chavvy clothes had
eclipsed any desire to go to university, and she had therefore
opted to spend the past five years stagnating at the local paper,
with all the other chavs who dressed like her and spoke like her
and made her feel as if she were in a home she couldn't leave. But
she knew too that to use a word like 'stagnating' would make it
seem as though she were showing off in front of Margaret, whose
life, just like her parents' lives, hadn't really provided much in the
way of opportunity. And then she tried and failed to be grateful
for the somewhat limited opportunities – in this case a made-up
course at the new FE college that she had joined for no other
reason than that it filled the empty hours suddenly gifted to her
courtesy of the British Army – that her own life presented now.

'Well I don't know if I'll ever get that far. But I would like to
move up from Swop Shop,' she said instead, while also trying to
ignore the fact that the swirling green pattern on the carpet was
beginning to make her feel sick.

'From Swop Shop?'

'It's the bit of the classifieds that I work on. The free ads section. People phone in with notices for things that they no longer
want and then say what they'd like to swop them for.' And then,
eager for a change of subject, she added, 'I got an email from Eoin
yesterday.'

'Can he send them too then? Even in the desert?'

'Yes of course. And Basra's on the coast.'

'Hail Queen of Heaven, the Ocean Star.'

'I'm sorry Margaret, what was that?'

'Hail Queen of Heaven – you must have heard it surely?'

Katarzyna nodded at the seething carpet and the telephone,

sunk in a tangle of wires, while simultaneously trying to remember the words to a hymn that she knew she must have sung but which, despite her efforts, continued to elude her. What did come back to her, however, was a fact that she had absorbed and retained, namely that the ocean, unlike the sea, was not where the water met the land, but where the water met the water, all of which meant that the Queen of Heaven therefore must be very far away, both from where Eoin was in Basra, and where she and Margaret waited for him . . .

'Well I'm glad to know that he's beside the seaside, and he has a dog too, you know. Now isn't that nice?' continued Margaret.

'A dog?'

'Yes, with a coat for when it gets cold.'

'But it's pretty hot out there. Over fifty degrees some days.'

'But Eoin is wearing sunscreen,' said Margaret, very definitely, as if that were the end of the matter, while Katarzyna, not knowing quite how to respond to this statement, put an entire biscuit in her mouth.

Meghana

MEGHANA BUDANNAVAR PLACED HER RUCKSACK on the empty chair beside her. She hoped that Kathy wasn't late, or alternatively, she hoped that Judy, the classified advertisements manager, wouldn't try to find a new friend for her in the meantime. Last month Judy had taken every available opportunity to seat her next to Aaeesha Begum, who also had brown skin; and yet to explain that Aaeesha came from Dhaka and Meghana came from Leicester, or that Aaeesha was a Muslim and Meghana was a Hindu (or more specifically Lingayat) seemed pointless, especially since her reluctance to place herself alongside the *Evening Post*'s only other brown person stemmed from the fact that Aaeesha had no discernible sense of humour, and didn't appear to understand the level of irony required in order to make it through the otherwise mundane day.

Meghana put on her headset and scanned the stuffy, strip-lit room, which by and large was populated either by disaffected school leavers, or over-tired, topping-up-their-income mums, plus anyone else who was prepared to work unusual hours for not much money. The Free Ads pages were as old as the paper itself, and probably the most pointless, being the only section that no one, bar those who placed the ads, or the students who occasionally prank-called them, ever read. Neither could the frequent references to Brian Clough's long-gone heyday, which all the other sections of the paper employed in an attempt to link 'old big head's' former glamour back to each and every piece of local news, be applied to a second-hand microwave, or indeed any of the other stranger and grubbier things to which their current owners hoped others could be persuaded to attach a value. It was pointless, Meghana silently repeated to herself, but it was also, from an ironical perspective, quite funny . . .

Meghana adjusted her headset so that it didn't press against her skull quite so tightly. She was pleased to see that Aaeesha had now been moved to Family Announcements, which, due to the paper's somewhat elderly demographic, tended more towards obituaries than weddings or babies, and that Judy's attention was currently taken up with one of their regular problem callers, who may or may not have also been the heavy breather who phoned Personal Services up to four or five times each day. That left only Sam from Motors, but although he paused, briefly, as he passed on his way to the kitchen, he registered the rucksack and moved on. She reached for a chocolate and then typed 'www.blueyonder.co.uk' into the navigation bar – except that the green light on the switchboard lit up before she had time to go any further. She clicked back to the Free Ads screen and pressed 'answer'.

'Hello, Evening Post Swop Shop. Meg speaking how can I help you?'

'Alright duck. Can you put that I've got two bags of items? And that I'd like to swop them for a plasma screen TV?'

Meghana began to type into one of the Free Ads boxes.

'And would you like to say a little bit more about your items?'

'You what duck?'

'Would you like to say a bit more about them? Experience has shown that our readers are more likely to do a swop if they know what your items actually are.'

'Oh right . . . ' The noise of heavy breathing now filled both of Meghana's ears. 'Just give me a minute, okay?'

'Take your time.'

Meghana looked up and waved at Kathy, who had just entered the office, and then pointed at the seat beside her.

'Err, okay duck, can you just say that they're assorted.'

'Assorted ... Yes.'

Meghana carried on typing into the Free Ads screen while Kathy removed her rucksack, put on her headset and then sat down.

'And can I take a name and number?'

'Sorry duck?'

'A name and telephone number so that the other readers can contact you about your items.'

'Oh okay, right. Let's say John, Mansfield 9835428.'

'Okay, *let's say* John,' she caught Kathy's eye, 'on Mansfield 9835428. Is that right?'

'Yes duck.'

'Okay I'll just read that back to you. Two bags of assorted items, will swop for plasma screen TV. Contact John, Mansfield 9835428. Is that right?'

'Yes duck.'

'It'll be in tomorrow night's paper. Thank you. Goodbye.'

Meghana pressed 'end call', and she and Kathy immediately burst out laughing. Then she clicked back to 'www.blueyonder. co.uk' while Kathy took one of the chocolates.

'Assorted items,' said Meghana, shaking her head. 'From *let's say* John.'

Kathy finished her chocolate, then grimaced at her sticky fingers.

'No one in their right mind is ever going to ring him up,' said Kathy.

'But there's a lot of people in their wrong minds,' said Meghana.

Meghana also took another chocolate, then put it back in the box again, and then considered what she'd just said. There's a lot of people in their wrong minds. There's a lot of people in their wrong minds in Mansfield and also Nottingham. There's a lot of people in their wrong minds in the City of Caves, which was also Nottingham, which was also the subject of her as yet unfinished anthropology doctorate, which she was undertaking in the geography department at the University of Nottingham because they had been able to offer her partial funding and were posher than Nottingham Trent. Silently, but still ironically, she began to recite the following words:

The City of Caves is a visitor attraction situated in Nottingham's Broadmarsh Shopping Centre. It consists of a network of caves carved out of sandstone, dating from the Dark Ages up until the 1960s. My study explores the attraction's impact on the political and narrative landscapes of the East Midlands area via the development of a counter-archaeological analysis. This involves reflection on previous archaeological findings and on the new heritage paradigm, and explores the complex materialities of people, places and objects, and the assemblages thereof . . .

As if reading her mind, Kathy said, 'And how's your PhD going?'

'Oh you know, same old, same old,' said Meghana, and then laughed awkwardly, because she always felt awkward whenever Kathy asked about her other life up at the university.

It made her remember that she had A Levels, a BSc and an MSc, and soon she'd have a PhD too. And then it made her remember that her parents were doctors and that Kathy's weren't, and then it made her forget that despite these differences they found the same things funny. She paused for a moment, then took back one of the chocolates and said, 'Well at the moment I'm looking at the way in which we experience physical things, or places, and how this shapes our consciousness—'

But the green light was flashing and Kathy, seeing Judy, pressed 'answer'.

'Hello, Evening Post Swop Shop . . .'

Meghana watched as Kathy carried on talking into the headset and typing into the boxes while also reaching for the chocolates.

'. . . Okay, so let me just read that back to you. Six bags of Arabian coffee, partially opened, will swop for kitchen appliances or children's toys. Contact Kylie, Nottingham 97344216. Is that right?' There was a pause during which Kathy clicked on a new window and then typed 'www.hotmail.com' into the navigation bar. 'It'll be in tomorrow night's paper. Thank you. Goodbye.'

'Partially opened?'

'Partially opened.'

Meghana laughed and then threw what remained of the chocolates into the wastepaper bin, where they ricocheted round the metal container. She clicked back to www.blueyonder.co.uk and typed 'meginthefield' into the username box and then 'megthefieldstudy' into the password box beneath it. She saw that there was one new message with a JPEG of her friend Dave in a wizard's hat attached to it, and then she looked over at Kathy's computer, where a photograph of Eoin, who resembled an old-fashioned film star, glimmered teasingly across the screen.

'But what about the way we experience other things?' said Kathy, who then looked back at her computer, where a message saying her message had been sent now hovered. 'Like the Internet?'

'But the Internet is virtual.'

'Yes, it's neither physical nor metaphysical. Isn't that what being virtual means?'

'And?'

'And what about the way we experience that?'

'Well ... I think that our experiences of virtual places are still dependent on the physical places that border them.'

'So the Internet isn't the ocean, it's the sea?'

Meghana took off her headset, shook out her hair, which she had begun to worry was her best feature, and then covered her locket with the palm of her hand.

'Yes. Or an airport. Or something.'

David

DR DAVID GOLDSTEIN PUT DOWN the battered paperback he'd
been reading and surveyed the sniggering boys in front of him,
then put another piece of nicotine gum in his mouth. He was still
trying to quit smoking, for the same reason that he had recently accepted the role of Games Workshop Manager and moved
back in with his parents; he needed to save money, and so he now
spent his days either herding teenagers around the shop, painting
Warhammer figures for the window display or else reading up on
the odd selection of science fiction novels and books of conspiracy theories that his colleague Paul left lying around.

David chewed slowly. It was precisely one year since he had
received his doctorate in *Religion and National Identity: Migrant
Communities in Nottingham*. His studies had taken place not in the
theology, but the geography department at the University of Nottingham, due to the full funding that was, at that time, still available. He had also held the coveted position of Cross-Cultural
Identities Research Group convener, and for this reason he had
enjoyed the respect of his peers. It had not been uncommon for
undergraduates to ask his advice on their essays, applications
and the like, one of whom had even included the line 'Dr [even
though he had not, at that point, been a Doctor] Goldstein is well
fit' within the any-other-comments box of the national student
survey. His supervisor had frequently introduced him as 'my star

pupil', and once even 'my successor'; and best of all, his contemporaries, meaning those who understood the nuances and cultural references associated with his age group, had regarded him as cool . . .

Remembering this, David looked down at the Stop the War Coalition badge he had deliberately pinned over the Games Workshop logo on his shirt, and then up at a boy covered in spots, who had detached himself from the rest of the group and was waiting, expectantly, for him.

'Excuse me but have you got any more Skaven? I can only see the ones in the display unit.'

David shook his head. 'We're all out I'm afraid. But we've still got elves, and err, dwarves – you know, everything else, we've got in.'

'But I really wanted Skaven.'

The boy looked at him pleadingly, as if his insistence combined with the shame of his spots would conjure a new box of figures, but all that David was able to offer in reply was another, more definite shake of the head. The mix of helplessness but also determination that he exuded reminded David, for the second time in as many minutes, of himself at that age. At eleven, he had won a scholarship to The High, a same-sex selective school in which he had thrived academically, although not socially, due to his being unable to disguise either his earnestness when it came to learning facts and figures, or his indifference to fashion and popular music – traits that his parents had, unwittingly, encouraged. His father, a now retired university professor and keen amateur cellist, had been delighted to have a son who, despite his tender years, enjoyed a Bach concerto. Likewise, his mother, a not quite retired professor, had demanded a similar level of intellectual engagement. She had refused either to make him packed lunches or to iron his clothes on the grounds that it would reinforce gender stereotyping, as had his father, on the grounds of being a gender, or perhaps merely academic, stereotype himself. As a result, David's teenage years had been crumpled ones, during which he had survived on Pot Noodles and remained oblivious to the Top 40, or indeed any other frame of reference that might have helped him to fit in. His social interactions were either with his parents' friends, or with other, similarly nerdy boys, with whom he played Battleships, then Dungeons and Dragons, then Warhammer – the inches, units and simulated conflicts appealing to his earnest facts-and-figures mind, and the different fantasy races simultaneously providing an escape from the confines of it ...

'What's this?'

David looked up and this time saw Meg standing on the other side of the counter. She must have entered without him realising, and was now holding up the same book that he had been reading earlier. It had a particularly lurid cover: orange and purple fractals adorned both the front and back, along with bold raised text that proclaimed 'THE KAOSPHERE', in which the 'a' was an anarchy symbol. He contemplated it for a moment, and then removed his piece of nicotine gum, stuck it under the counter and said, 'Err, well, it's about a kind of occult anti-system in which eight arrows representing all possibilities, and one arrow, representing the, err, the single, certain road of Law—'

'No I meant what's this.'

And he saw that she was also holding one of the miniature figures. 'Oh that's Tzeentch, the god of change, fate, mutation, hope and, err, knowledge.'

'And he lives in the Kaosphere?'

'Well according to the packaging he lives in the Warp, although as the Kaosphere is supposed to encompass all possibilities I suppose he, err, well, I suppose that he could live there too.'

David took Tzeentch from her, noticing as he did so that the enamel was still a little tacky, and then positioned him, very carefully, on the edge of the counter. He watched as Meg prodded his little tableau with the tip of her long, elegant finger, and then almost disdainfully said, 'I can't imagine why anyone would want to buy him.'

'Then you need to work on your imagination. He's one of our best sellers, although he never does quite as well as the, err, the Skaven.'

'The mice people?'

'Yes,' he said, even though he knew that really they were anthropomorphic rat men, 'the mice people.'

'You don't sound very enthusiastic.'

'That's probably because I'm not very enthusiastic.'

'And why have you put a badge on your nipple?'

David looked down and laughed, removing his Stop the War Coalition badge to reveal the Games Workshop's logo.

'Oh,' said Meg.

'Yes. Oh. And why aren't you wearing yours? Or don't you want to stop the war?'

'No, no of course I do, it's just that I, you know, I felt awkward in front of Kathy . . .'

But rather than continue with her excuses she put Paul's copy of *The Kaosphere* back down on the counter, and then attempted to reposition the little blue figure so that it was standing on top of it and Tzeentch appeared to be rising up out of the fractals. As soon as his foot touched the 'a' however, a loud crash emanated from the front of the shop. The shelving unit, which had been badly put together and overladen with boxes, had collapsed into the display unit, and the remaining Gods of Demonic Chaos fell, together with all of the other iron miniatures, onto the Games Workshop floor. Instinctively Meg grabbed David's arm, and then, almost instinctively, David pulled her towards him.

'It looks like a bomb exploded,' said Meg, poking her toe at the cubes of safety glass that glittered all around them. 'Or else something from a science fiction movie.'

'Err, yes,' said David.

He leaned forward and, immediately reverting to his usual fumblings, attempted to remove a wooden splinter from her hair.

'Or perhaps the, err, the Warp.'

Stanisław

STANISŁAW KWIATKOWSKI STROLLED PAST THE display unit, and towards Dave who, now that he had said goodbye to Meg had resumed reading *The Kaosphere*. He wore a bright, tight-fitting yellow tee-shirt, on which the image of shattering glass – and underneath it the words 'In Case of Emergency Break *Dance*' – strained, like the skin of an overripe melon, across his ample stomach. As he looked at the hazard tape, which had been dramatically wrapped around the broken shelves, it occurred to him that it was the same waspish colour scheme as he was. Consequently, upon reaching the counter he smiled, pointed at his chest and then the tape and said, 'Matchie, matchie.'

'Oh, yes, yes. I see what you mean and, err—'

'You are Mr Dave, yes? You called me about the broken shelves.'

'Well I'm Mr Goldstein actually, or even Dr Goldstein, but I mean I'm also Dave. I mean just call me Dave and, err ...'

Stanisław laughed so that the gold teeth at the back of his mouth now showed, and then banged his toolbox down between them, but before Dave had time to say anything else a boy with the beginnings of a moustache came over.

'Excuse me but have you got any more Skaven?'

'You're in luck,' said Dave, producing a new box from underneath the till. 'We had a delivery this morning which—'

'You buy this?' Stanisław interrupted. 'But meant for child, yes?'

23

The boy looked nervous.

'But you are not child, yes?'

'I'm fourteen.'

'Fourteen.' Again Stanisław's laugh rang out around the room. 'You are man now, yes?'

'But it's a war game,' said Dave, giving the boy a smile. 'It involves, you know, tactics.'

'But Dr Dave,' said Stanisław, his large, pink finger prodding playfully at Dave's nipple, 'you want to stop the war, yes?'

He watched as Dr Dave (who he knew full well was really just plain Dave or else, should he genuinely want to be formal as opposed to merely facetious, Mr Goldstein) laughed, and then began to ring the Skaven through the till. As soon as he had done so the boy grabbed the box and all but ran out of the shop. Dave followed him to the door, and then locked it. Through the window was a large group of young women with bare legs, drinking alcopops and stumbling towards the Market Square, giggling and shrieking as they went . . .

'This is great city,' said Stanisław suddenly, flinging his fat, pink arms out wide and so revealing the two dark circles of sweat that lurked beneath them. 'Perhaps greatest city I will ever know.'

'And have you known many others? Besides this great one?' said Dave, putting the key back in his pocket.

'I have known also Skegness, for the mini-breaks. And city of my birth, which is Gdańsk.'

'Gdańsk?' And, as Dave turned back round to face him, a note of curiosity entered his voice. 'That's a very beautiful place to, err . . .'

Stanisław opened his toolbox, found a bag of nails and started placing them between his lips.

'If you say beautiful, you do not know Gdańsk.'

'But, err—'

'You do not know Gdańsk,' Stanisław repeated, apparently unhindered by the nails. 'But I do know Gdańsk. Which is why I leave, twenty-three years ago, and not one single day do I look back.'

'But how?' And again Dave's tone betrayed his curiosity, while making reference, however implicit, to the fact that it would not have been easy, or legal, to leave a country that had, at that time, sealed its borders. 'What I mean is, well, it must have been kind of hard to leave what with the, err, the, err, political situation and, err ...'

'If you really want to leave the place then you will find the ways to leave the place.'

'But, err ...'

But, rather than explain how his then pregnant, then teenage wife, who had been selected, by what now seemed like providence, to take part in a state-sponsored cultural excursion to the west, had had the foresight, when she got there, to seek asylum, and the numerous appeals, forgeries and bribes that had followed in his desperate attempts to join her, Stanisław turned away. He knelt on the floor beside the remnants of the shelving unit, placed his thumb and index finger around one of the nails as if it were a cigarette and, positioning it over the first board, said, 'It is good to have the beer. Even when you are working, it is sometimes good to have the beer.'

Dave looked at the nail uncertainly.

'Would you, err, would you like a beer?'

'Yes Dave. The beer would be good. The beer would help to make the party.'

Dave looked, uncertainly, at the nail again, and then back at Stanisław again, and then finally disappeared into the storeroom, before returning, a moment later, with two small bottles of beer. He uncapped them both with a gadget on his key-ring and handed one to Stanisław.

'So what did you, err, what did you do in Gdańsk? I mean were you an, err, an odd-job – I mean were you an, err ...'

'I work in shipyards.'

'In the shipyards?'

Stanisław was not looking at Dave, but Dave's eager, curious tone, now ten times brighter than before, betrayed the extent of his curiosity far better than any physical expression could have done, and yet Stanisław was reluctant to indulge him. Instead he raised the bottle to his lips, and then, still without meeting Dave's eye, drained its contents. He already knew, exactly, what kind of story Dave had attached to his past, and what kind of romantic struggles he wanted Stanisław to relate to him, in his husky, heavily accented voice. The stories of hardship, told as if photographed in black and white, of murdered priests whose faces were now immortalised on sets of highly collectable postage stamps, of the unions, Solidarność, Wałęsa and any other word that could be said with one's clenched fist in the air . . .

'The shipyards is bad place,' said Stanisław curtly, and on the word 'bad' he simultaneously slammed down the bottle and hit the first nail, very squarely, on the head. 'No one want to sit next to smelly workers on the public transportation. I do not miss shipyard. I do not feel what you want me to feel.'

'But you must feel something?'

Yes of course I feel something, thought Stanisław, driving in another nail and then another, namely that there is nothing ennobling about B.O., but he had already tried and failed to put this into words and besides, who wanted to sully a bright sunny day filled with laughing, bare-legged young women with the dirty grey soot of the past? He reached for his bottle again before remembering that it was empty, and then, looking out into the now empty street and then back at Dave, he said, 'I think we are nearly ready for another beer now, yes?'

31.08.2004

The first incentive was a phone. A Nokia, pay-as-you-go with £10 credit. The second was £200. Then another £200 when training finished. I thought: That's better than McDonald's, count me in. Except out here it doesn't work. No reception.

Feudalism

STANISŁAW KWIATKOWSKI PRESSED THE DOORBELL and waited. Then he pressed it again. And again. And then he remembered that he was there to fix the doorbell and felt stupid, all the more so since it was a Sunday morning and he was wearing a shirt and tie. His wife, Iwona, put one hand on his arm, which had been her usual sign for him to stop whatever he was doing ever since they had first started dating, while his daughter bent down until her face was level with the letterbox, pushed it open and shouted, 'Margaret are you there? Margaret it's me, it's Kathy I've—'

'Is that you Kathy?' came a voice from inside the house.

'Yes it's me Margaret, I've brought my dad to fix the bell.'

'Is that you Stan?'

'Yes Margaret, I am Stan.'

'And there is also me Margaret, Iwona,' said Iwona, who then smoothed her hair in the same brusque, efficient way she had always done. 'You need have no concern.'

From inside the house came the noise of several keys twisting in several locks and a large, heavy bolt being pulled back, and a moment later Margaret herself appeared.

'Oh well this is grand, just grand. Now please, please you must all come in.'

Stanisław stepped inside. As he did so he saw the calendar (which was now on September, meaning more roses and

fewer crosses), the plates on the wall and the elaborately patterned furniture; indeed, the only real difference, as far as he
could see, between Margaret's home and theirs was that his wife
had hung a picture of Pope John Paul II in the exact same spot
that Margaret had placed Our Lady. Noticing this last detail he
stopped and bowed his head, an action that alerted him to his
too-tight collar.

'Don't you think that dad looks smart?' said Katarzyna, as
Stanisław began to tug at his top button.

'Oh yes Stan. Yes of course. You're a fine figure of a man you
know,' said Margaret.

'But my family call me a fat man.' And in spite of her protestations Stanisław burst out laughing. Once more he tugged at his
collar, while the three women stared into the carpet's swirls, until
the guilt finally overcame him and, after tucking his tie inside his
shirt, he pointed to a patch of wall above the door. 'I have located
source of your problem Margaret,' he said, gesturing to an exposed inch of wire, 'and you will be pleased to know that it is the
simple one to fix.'

'Oh Stan I am glad, but only if it's no trouble. Now can I get
you all a cup of tea?'

'No, no we are all fine for the teas thank you Margaret,' said
Stanisław, and then, almost hopefully, 'and I suppose it is too
early for the beer?'

'Oh well I don't really drink beer Stan but—'

'The teas would be very nice Margaret,' Iwona cut in. 'Kasia
will help you to prepare the teas now, yes?'

Margaret nodded and shuffled off into the kitchen, with
Katarzyna dutifully in tow. Stanisław then turned off the electricity, removed a penknife from his pocket and began to strip the
wires. It was an easy enough job, and within a matter of seconds,
or so it seemed, he had joined them together again, turned the
electricity back on, and was sitting, heavily, on the settee where,
straight away, the cushions began to conspire against him.

'I'm glad that you're helping Margaret,' said Iwona, in Polish,
and then in spite of this not being a language that Margaret spoke

29

she paused and lowered her voice. 'It must be hard for her now that Eoin isn't here.'

Her manner, which wanted, yet refused to be, entirely tender, was one that Stanisław knew well. It was the manner of those who would rather feel sorry for other people than be the victim of pity themselves, and of those who had grown up with nothing, yet considered it vulgar to mention this fact. He had met Iwona one week after the 1979 Ms Gdańsk pageant, at which she had been awarded second place before going straight back to work at the factory that also employed his cousin. Iwona should have come first in his opinion, and might have done so had she joined the Party – except that like him she had a heart and a brain. What good was a better flat when no one decent would want to come and visit you in it? Or better food when no one you liked would want to eat it with you? And then of course they were both Catholics, who had listened to the Holy Father; 'Be not afraid' was what he had said . . .

So Iwona had continued to work on the production line, making tractor parts with all of the other intelligent, uneducated women. And then, because they were young, and she was beautiful, and both had hearts as well as brains, they got married. And made a home together. And had a child together. And stayed together just as the Holy Father had instructed them to do. And the love that they still shared, after all these years, was shaped by gratitude and stoicism and faith, as much as habit . . .

'Well it's hard for everyone,' began Stanisław, gripping the armrest. 'But it's not as if—'

He stopped at the sound of what he assumed was crockery being taken out the cupboard, and a moment later Margaret shuffled back into the room, weighed down by a tray of cups and saucers. Katarzyna, who was following behind, pulled out one of the tables from the nest in the corner and helped Margaret set everything down, somewhat shakily, upon it, then arranged herself on one of the chairs.

As soon as she was settled Iwona said, 'And you have heard from Eoin yes? Kasia sends the electronic letters.'

'Soon she'll be a famous journalist,' said Margaret, proudly.

'Unless she gets married,' said Stanisław, dully.

Katarzyna shot him a pointed look, picked up the teapot and said, 'They're called emails.' She poured out a cup and handed it to Margaret, and then a second one for Stanisław, thus forcing him to loosen his grip on the armrest, and veer, even further, towards the settee's depths, while trying not to spill tea upon his trousers.

Iwona, meanwhile, had already turned her attention back towards Margaret. Smiling at her, she said, 'Yes, soon I will start to make the dress. I will make the long, white dress for church. And also the veil of netting.'

'And which church will that be Kathy? The Polish Church or . . . ?'

'The Polish Church,' said Iwona, and then, 'or maybe even the Cathedral.'

'The Cathedral,' said Margaret, beaming at all three of them. 'Now wouldn't that be grand?'

'Yes,' said Iwona, very firmly. 'The Cathedral would be very nice, yes.'

Suddenly, however, another of the settee's cushions began to slip away from Stanisław, and seeing this he punched it back into place in such a way that all three women started. Then he took a large gulp of tea, thinking as he did so that it had been made with too much water and not enough lemons or leaves or, in Polish, that it lacked 'esencja', then he began to swill it around his mouth like mouthwash in the hope that this would increase the taste. As he did so he looked out of the window where autumn was already beginning. He saw that the leaves were dying, and that the trees would soon be bare; and then he wondered what anyone, least of all his Kasia, could possibly see in Eoin O'Shea?

Militarism

MARGARET O'SHEA WALKED INTO ST Flannan's with what would have been a spring in her step if it hadn't been for the ache in her knees. To the casual observer the church, which was both dingy and sparse, would not have appeared to be anything special, but for those who had had been there since its inception it was a thing of beauty pure.

When Margaret had first come over, at the end of the 1960s, there hadn't been anywhere on The Meadows estate for her or any of the other Catholics, meaning Irish, to pray. Every week they'd had to walk to the Cathedral, and put a little of their little in the plate. But afterwards they'd had another collection, and then another, until eventually they'd saved enough to buy a piece of land, and pay an architect to make a plan. Until all those good strong Irish hands that had worked so hard to build the English roads had built an Irish church. And not just any church – St Flannan's!

It was the first time since Eoin had been away that anyone had accompanied Margaret to mass there, but now here she was, not only with Kathy, who was pretty, and Iwona, who was smart, but also Stan, a fine, fine figure of a man who, just like her late husband, Steven, had worked in a shipyard (although the less said about what had happened to Steven there the better).

Margaret squeezed Stanisław's hand, and said hello to Blessings, and then to one or two of the Rwandan ladies, before finally greeting Danny and Padraig and Sinead. She'd met all three of them at the Irish Centre the very first day that she and her daughter had arrived in Nottingham, and although they had all come from other places – Derry, Antrim and, in Sinead's case, another, not so different, suburb of Belfast – they had all immediately taken her to be what they were too: survivors. She could see that Sinead was in the process of putting the hymnbooks back on the little wooden trolley, but as soon as she noticed Margaret she straight away stopped what she was doing and smiled.

'Well goodness me Margaret,' she said, admiringly. 'It looks like you've brought quite a crowd.'

Margaret whistled, picked up one of the hymnbooks, and nodded, first of all, at Kathy.

'Well this here is Eoin's fiancée, Kathy, and Kathy this is Sinead.'

Sinead turned to her, and said, 'Good to meet you Kathy. We've all been remembering Eoin in our prayers.'

'That's very kind. Thank you.'

'And this here is her mother, Iwona,' Margaret continued, 'and her father, Stan, who has been doing great work fixing my doorbell.'

'Hello Yvonne,' said Sinead, now turning to Iwona, and then, 'Sounds like you're a good man to have about the house Stanley.'

Stan tugged at the collar of his shirt.

'I am good man, yes. So tell me, why have my family decided to put this noose around my neck?'

Sinead looked confused and Margaret quickly said, 'They're Polish,' which was her way of saying without saying that Stan's behaviour was because he was foreign as opposed to rude or strange, and then, 'and they live in Sneinton,' which was her way of saying that although they'd never been to St Flannan's before they were still nice, good, church-going Catholics.

'Ah so I see . . .' said Sinead, which was her way of saying without saying that she understood. 'So I see Margaret, so I see.'

Margaret checked her watch which, unlike the clock at home, was silent and so did not remind her quite so explicitly of the irregularities of her heart. She could already hear the organ beginning to groan, and see the two new black altar boys fidgeting beside it. She knew that Father Jonathan had picked these particular boys to be altar boys because Danny, God bless him, had refused to shake their mother's hand due to its darker colour; and yet she also knew that it would be wrong to be too hard on Danny just because, even if it came out a bit skew-whiff sometimes, he was protective of all they'd fought for . . .

'So we go in now Margaret, yes?'

'Oh yes Iwona. Yes of course.'

Stan again held out his arm, which Margaret was pleased to take hold of, and the four of them went inside and found four seats right up at the front together. As soon as they sat down Margaret took off her hearing aid and put it in her pocket – because it wasn't as if she didn't already know when to stand, or sit, or kneel, or when to stand again, just as she already knew the words to all the hymns, and when to put her money in the little wicker basket, and when to expect the rustle of 'peace be with you' followed by communion . . .

Margaret stood up, ready and waiting to go through all the motions, which to her were so much more than motions, until, forgetting her hearing aid and thus forgetting the tune, she burst into quavering song. And as she sang she looked at Kathy, and Stan and Iwona; and Danny and Padraig and Sinead; and one of the new black ladies from Rwanda, whose boys were now altar boys; and the new black lady from Malawi who was called Blessings; and then last of all she looked at the statue of Mary, which this time was life-size, and had a little red light placed at the bottom of its painted plaster feet that, regardless of the day or night, was always burning.

Votus

DR DAVID GOLDSTEIN PUT ON his jacket and, as an afterthought, slipped *The Kaosphere* into his pocket. If pressed he would have been forced to admit that it was rather a poorly written, perhaps even superficial piece of literature, and yet the idea it explored, that there was no purpose or grand cosmic scheme to life beyond what one chose to believe, struck him not so much as cynical, but freeing. With this in mind he said goodbye to his parents, both of whom mumbled something back at him from behind the Sunday papers, and then let himself out of the house, walking up through West Bridgford and towards the city centre, where he was meeting Meg, supposedly for brunch, but actually for drinks that started early.

Although he had only ever intended the move back home, like the job at Games Workshop, to be temporary, he knew deep down that things were already too comfortable. As he passed through West Bridgford and into The Meadows, which had always struck him as an ugly part of town, he thought about how much the house he'd grown up in, like all of the other houses in that part of Nottingham, differed from the buildings that now surrounded him. His parents' house was detached, and had a garage and a garden. Inside, it was painted in pale Farrow & Ball colours, and had framed posters from classical music concerts on the walls. He wondered, in the liberal-minded manner of the liberal-minded middle classes, just what it would be like to live in one of these dense, low-ceilinged buildings, and to be dependent not on his mum and dad but on the council. In some ways it struck him as a romantic way to live because it complemented the view of working-class and immigrant life that had informed his doctoral studies and in some ways it was easy to picture himself, the former Cross-Cultural Identities Group convener, staring out across the crumbling satellite dishes with Moleskine notebook, fountain pen and *The Kaosphere* in hand . . . But in reality he knew that he preferred to view the scene from the shadows of academia, and that were he ever to see this portrait, that he had painted in the fading light, up close and personal, then he would also see the cracks that marked the oil's surface.

'Dave!' came a loud foreign voice from behind him. Then, even more insistently, 'Dave! Davc! Daaave!'

David turned round, but the only people he could see were a large, fat man in a tight shirt and tie, an old lady he took to be the man's mother and a surprisingly smart-looking woman he assumed must be someone else's wife. The three of them were standing in front of a church, which, like everything else in the immediate vicinity, was built from a serviceable yellow brick, and which he knew from his case studies must be St Flannan's – but still he couldn't place them.

'Dave?'

This time it was a woman's voice, and when he turned the other way he saw Kathy. Instinctively he raised his right hand to cover his Stop the War Coalition badge, and waved awkwardly at her with his left.

As if registering his confusion, Kathy said, 'We've just been to mass.' And then, going over to join the trio, she half-pointed at the smart-looking woman, 'This is my mum.'

'Hello,' said David.

'And this is my dad.'

David nodded automatically, before registering who it was.

'I'm sorry I didn't, err—'

But Stan was already slapping him, a little too hard, on the back.

'You recognise me now, yes Dr Dave? Even without my funny tee-shirt?'

'Yes, yes of course, I just wasn't, err, I just wasn't expecting to—'

'And this is Margaret,' Kathy continued, as if it was perfectly natural that he and Stan should know each other. 'Margaret is Eoin's grandma.'

'Oh, err, right, err, hi ...'

Stan delivered another slap to David's back and said, 'You are ready for the beer, yes Dave?'

'Well, actually yes. I mean I'm already going for one actually. With my, err, with my, err, my friend, Meg.' He looked back at Kathy again. 'But I mean I'm sure she'd love to see you too. I mean, yeah you're welcome to join us. Both of you. All of you, err ...'

'Kasia, Dave is asking you out for the beer,' said Stan.

'Well it's more like brunch really,' said David.

'Brunch?' said Iwona, perking up. 'The brunch sounds very nice.' But then catching Margaret's eye she added, 'Although perhaps you wait and go for the brunch with Eoin?'

'Well, err ...' said David.

'I mean I wouldn't want to intrude,' said Kathy.

'But you really wouldn't be in the way,' said David, who was suddenly very keen to leave them all and, having never thought that he would actually be expected to expand upon his offer, now very much regretted it. 'I mean, all of you. You're all very welcome. Please, err, please come.'

'Actually ...' said Kathy, pulling up the zipper on her tracksuit top. 'I think that I will come with you. Just for one.'

'Oh, err, right,' said David.

'Good. Good. Live your life!' shouted Stan.

'But the teas?' said Iwona.

'More teas?' said Margaret.

Kathy bent down and kissed Margaret on the cheek, then ran off across the church car park before Iwona had time to stop her. David watched, almost admiringly, as she leapt over a small clump of shrubbery and into the road, before remembering that he was meant to be going with her. For a moment he remained where he was, standing stupidly between the various members of her family until, figuring there was nothing else for it, he also started running.

'So how come you know my dad?' said Kathy, when he eventually caught up with her.

David stopped and took a few deep breaths, filling up what were still smoker's lungs.

'He came to fix some stuff for us up at the Games Workshop. I didn't realise he was your dad though, even though you're both Kwiat ... Kwiaro—'

'Kwiatkowski, or ska. It's a bit like Smith in Polish. Except that in Polish it means flowers.'

Kathy Flowers, thought David, patting his pockets in search of his nicotine gum. Kathy Flowers, who lived in Forest Fields, where Meg, a former Cross-Cultural Identities Group attendee, also lived, as a tourist. Kathy Flowers, who wore a pink velvet tracksuit and went to church in The Meadows.

'Flowers in the meadows and the forests and the fields,' he said, without thinking, and then, worried in case she thought that he was coming on to her, he quickly added, 'I'm sure Meg will be pleased to see you.'

'Oh yeah, yeah I want to talk to her about the caves.'

'The, err ...? Oh yes, the caves.'

'It's funny, I always used to think of caves as being exclusive to Nottingham somehow, but since, you know, the Middle East and everything, I always picture the battle of Tora Bora,' Kathy continued, blithely.

'I'm not sure that I follow ...?'

'When the American troops first went into Afghanistan? Everyone was convinced that Osama bin Laden was hiding in a complex of caves that ran underneath the mountains.'

'Oh yeah. Yeah of course.'

'It's funny to talk about a complex of caves isn't it? It sounds like the caves have emotional problems.'

38

'Yes I suppose so.'

'Or actually no. It sounds like the mountains have emotional problems and their emotional problems have taken the form of a fixation upon the caves.'

'Err ...'

Dave half swallowed his piece of nicotine gum, and then spat it out again, while Kathy, seemingly oblivious to this fact, wittered on. He held the wet squidgy blob in his hand and then, when he was sure that she wasn't looking, dropped it into the gutter. Momentarily he felt ashamed, but at the same time also pleased, to be rid of the gum. He was looking forward to seeing Meg, who had always been able to discuss abstract concepts in a sensible, practical way, as opposed to the touchy feely kind of conversation that was taking place now. It made him remember that Kathy was a conventionally beautiful woman and that he was a geek, where-as Meg was a geek, who also happened to be beautiful – and thinking of this, he smiled.

'And you don't have to hide your badge Dave,' said Kathy, smiling back at him. 'I'm the last person that wants this war.'

Heresy

KATARZYNA KWIATKOWSKA CARRIED ON SPEAKING her thoughts out loud. This was partly because it was such a relief to be rid of them, to clear out her overcrowded brain which, ever since Eoin had gone, had gradually filled up with the pointless trivia of *The Post* and of New College, and then mixed it all up together in an ever-rising panic; and partly because she couldn't have said them to her parents, who wouldn't have understood, or worse still to any of her friends, meaning Meg, who might have. Dave was different though, in that he seemed sympathetic but also slightly distant, as well as being the only man besides her father who was able to look at her and not her breasts.

Katarzyna thought and spoke simultaneously about the start of her name, 'kwiatow', which meant flowers, and also the end of her name, 'ska', which meant that she, in the feminine sense, belonged to it. Which meant that she was the daughter of flowers, or more simply, that she was of flowers. Katarzyna Daughter of Flowers. Or Katarzyna of Flowers. Either way it made her sound like a saint, or The Virgin, all of which sounded very romantic and poetic but also very far away from her life at the *Evening Post*, or her life at New College, or what had, until recently, been her life with Eoin. In fact, whenever she thought about what had, until recently, been her life with Eoin she ached, physically, for it in a way that wasn't remotely flowery or saintly or virginal, just as she ached for it now . . .

'So do you always go to Church?' said Dave.

'What? No. Only sometimes.'

'And the church in The Meadows, St Flannan's, that's Margaret's church?'

'Yes.'

'And which church do you go to when you sometimes go?'

'Well I'm a fan of Gothic Revival so I like the Cathedral,' said Kathy. And then because she was aware that Dave was the sort of middle-class man who might assume she wasn't really clever, she added, 'Gothic Revival is a Victorian version of the middle ages.'

'Oh. Err, right, well . . .'

Katarzyna did up the zipper on her tracksuit top, thinking that what she had meant by being a fan of a Victorian version of the middle ages was that she was a fan of fiction and horror and death – and sometimes romance too – except that, once again, she didn't quite dare to say so out loud. Because despite leaving school at sixteen, or even before leaving school at sixteen, she had filled her absorbent, retentive, then not so overcrowded brain with novels from the classics section of Sneinton library, which was mostly Gothic literature with Caspar David Friedrich reproductions on the covers. They had all been set in dramatic, not-too-unbelievable landscapes, which one could imagine translating, very easily, into film. When she had exhausted the fiction section she moved on to art and architecture, and general histories of both the Victorian period and whatever sections of the even more distant past it wished to ape, and she knew that having encountered these books outside of school she was free to indulge her intelligence and the melancholy daydreams that it produced to the full. Or alternatively to enjoy them.

Katarzyna continued to pull, absently, at her zipper, because if everyone was always going to think of her as some sort of chav then she might as well dress the part, even if it annoyed her mother, especially if she was going with her to church. She thought about the last time Eoin had called her; she'd been in the bath, which meant that he'd had to leave a message, which she had then played back, over and over again, listening to him state who he was and how he would try again later, and then just before he hung up: 'I miss you Kathy.'

Except that he had said, 'I miss you Katheh.' Because he had grown up in the same place she had.

Katarzyna continued to pull, absently, at her zipper, still, and remembered how, after listening to the message, she had touched her cheek the way he used to, and shut her eyes and pretended. First, that she was lying with her face buried in the warmth of his armpit, except that because it was his armpit, it wasn't gross, and then that they were talking to each other. Botany and zoology had never really interested her, but she liked to listen to Eoin talk about them because of the care and passion that resonated in his voice when he did. She loved the way he said her name with an accent that, like her own, was generally seen as common, even though he had a way of saying things, and seeing things, that wasn't common at all. She remembered all of this, and kept on remembering, until after ten days the message had been automatically deleted – and how much longer could she pretend that he was here?

'What's that?' she said, pointing at the book in Dave's back pocket.

'This?' He took out *The Kaosphere*, and then, rather awkwardly, handed it to her, 'It's called *The*, err, *Kaosphere*.'

'And what's it about?'

'Well ... it's about a kind of occult anti-system in which eight arrows representing all possibilities, and one—' He stopped abruptly. 'Actually it's about magik – with a "k".'

'Oh right. So like, serious magik?'

'Postmodern magik.'

'Which is?'

'The belief that belief itself is a tool, an active force. It means that you can choose what to believe or not to believe depending on what system will best serve you at any particular time.'

'So I could be a Christian one day and a Muslim the next?'

'Yes. Or the Games Workshop Manager one day, and an almighty wizard the next. Or a PhD nerd one day and the world's greatest lover the next. Or—'

'But what if I can't find anything that I want to believe in?'

'Well you don't have to just go from one religion, or occupation, to another. You can mix and match. The Kaosphere represents a kind of collage almost. You could take parts from Christianity, Islam, Jedi, even Tzeentch—'

'What?'

'It doesn't matter. But you could take parts from all of these other religions, or science fictions or fantasies, or romances even, their beliefs and rituals, and then create new beliefs and rituals for each occasion. It doesn't matter where they come from or how often they change as long as you believe it when you do it.'

I believe in you, thought Katarzyna, thinking of Eoin. I believe that I remember you. I believe that I will continue to remember you and I believe that you will continue to remember me . . .

'. . . And the best thing about it is that we, the magicians, don't even have to inhabit the same physical space anymore. Lots of people use Skype or even email to communicate with each other. In fact, I read about a ritual performed by a group of magicians, one of whom was in the UK, one of whom was in Germany, and one of whom was actually in the middle of the ocean but who, between them, had managed to utilise a series of electronic devices which—'

'Or even email?'

'Yeah or video conferencing or text messaging or . . .'

But Katarzyna was no longer listening. Instead she adjusted her baseball cap and pulled up the zipper on her pink velvet tracksuit that matched her full, pink mouth and laughed, not because any one specific thing was funny but because she was delighted. Because she believed in Eoin and she believed in belief and two and two made four or five or whatever else you chose to believe ... And then Dave, who she suspected also longed to escape the mundane reality of this, their present moment, laughed too.

The Trip to Jerusalem

MEGHANA BUDANNAVAR WAITED IN YE Olde Trip to Jerusalem (or the Trip to Jerusalem as it was more widely known, or The Trip if you were local), a pub that was famous for three things. Firstly, having been established in the tenth century, it claimed to be the oldest pub in England (hence Ye Olde); secondly, the crusaders had, supposedly, stopped by (or in ye olde English 'tripped'); and thirdly most of the rooms had been carved out of the soft sandstone rock that rose up out of the hillsides on the city's edges, so that sitting, waiting, in The Trip was indistinguishable from sitting, waiting, in a cave filled with armchairs and beer.

Meghana went up to the bar. The only other person besides herself was a man in an England shirt who was on his third pint already. He was watching the football on a flashy-looking mobile that Meghana, noticing his missing front tooth, began to wonder if he might have stolen.

'A gin and tonic please,' she said to the barman, and upon hearing her voice the man in the England shirt turned round.

His eyes flitted briefly over her body, the shape of which was emphasised by a dress so bright and colourful that no one would notice anything but it, and then further adorned with her Stop the War Coalition badge, which she had worn, even though it didn't really go with the dress, just to keep Dave quiet. The man in the England shirt's eyes moved up, towards her face, and then held her gaze for a second before sneering, and turning away.

Meghana took her drink from the barman, and returned to her seat and waited. She could feel that the man in the England shirt was still watching her, and, not wanting it to appear as if she was intimidated by him, she took a sip of her drink. And then another, and so on, so that by the time Dave arrived she was already tipsy.

'I ran into Kathy on the way,' said Dave, motioning to the figure, who, Meg now saw, was standing in the doorway behind him. 'So can I get you a drink then Meg – oh I see that you've already got one, or do you want another one? And, err, can I get—'

'Actually let me get you both a drink,' said Kathy.

'Oh, yes, okay, a pint of bitter would be great,' said Dave, and then wriggled round the table until he was sitting very close to Meghana, who was now watching Kathy, as she approached the bar, and the man in the England shirt who had now switched his attention to Kathy's breasts.

'You know Kathy's actually alright,' said Dave, following her gaze.

'Because she's attractive?' said Meghana.

'No, because she's clever. In a kind of weird, self-educated way.'

Kathy is attractive, and clever in a kind of weird, self-educated way, thought Meghana, and then felt the weight of her hair and the indignity of her dress, whereas I have worn clothes so awful that they have eclipsed my one good feature ... She looked up at the decrepit model ship above the bar, which, if local folklore was to be believed, would cause anyone who touched it to drop down dead; and then recalled what, at one point, had nearly been her thesis:

The Nottingham Ghost Walk is the city's most successful walking tour, centring on the history of England's oldest public house, Ye Olde Trip to Jerusalem. My study explores the concept of the 'moving tourist attraction' and its attempts to reimagine the emotional and narrative landscapes of the East Midlands area ...

The more she thought about it, the more unsure she became as to whether her actual thesis topic was more or less boring than this other one that she had previously rejected; and then she became even more irritated by the fact that they, like everything else in her life, were probably more or less the same. She could see that Kathy was now trying her best to escape from the man in the England shirt, gradually edging away from the bar, and back over towards where she and Dave were sitting. Then, as soon as she reached them she placed one pink velvet thigh on either side of the stool and, still holding all their drinks, sat down, at which point the man in the England shirt shouted: 'Lucky seat!'

'Okay, thanks for that,' said Kathy.

The three of them sipped their drinks in silence, and then Kathy smiled at Meghana and said, 'Dave's been telling me all about postmodern magik – with a "k".'

'Oh really?' said Meg, trying not to sound as angry and pointless as she felt, 'Did he mention the Skaven too? They're anthropomorphic mice people.'

'Rat men,' said Dave.

'Rat toys,' said Meghana.

The three of them sipped their drinks again, in silence again, waiting for the alcohol to make things easier, and then after a minute or so Kathy said, 'So our pal at the bar just told me that that old ship is meant to be haunted?'

'Yes. Apparently if you touch it, or more particularly clean it, then you'll die immediately,' said Meghana.

'Well I've heard it doesn't even have to be you touching it. It could just be someone close to you, or the next person that you, err, touched,' said Dave.

'Anyway it's all rubbish. Nobody really believes it,' said Meghana.

Kathy shivered, and pulled up the zipper on her tracksuit top.

'I believe it. I'm a Romantic, and I believe in belief.'

Dave laughed awkwardly.

'Well I don't,' Meghana said. 'I'm an anthropologist and I study the science of humans and their works.' And then, emboldened by her gin and tonics, she stood up and made her way towards the bar.

'Meg don't do it!' said Dave, still laughing.

'No Meg don't,' said Kathy, her face turning pale.

'Don't be stupid,' said Meghana, 'it's just a dirty old ship, that's all.'

She clambered onto one of the stools and reached her right hand out, slowly and dramatically, towards the sails, and as she did so the man in the England shirt's eyes locked onto hers, then moved all over her. The whites had a yellow tinge from drinking, as did his skin, and there were drops of sweat on his forehead. She looked at him and raised her eyebrows.

'What?'

Meghana's right hand was now touching the top of the ship, while her left was balled into a fist. The man in the England shirt continued to stare, opening and closing his unkempt mouth, until Meghana jumped down off the stool and walked triumphantly away. She sat back down with Dave and Kathy and laughed and drank more of her drink and said, 'See? I'm still here. No one died.'

'Err, right . . .' said Dave, looking at the space above her head.

Meghana swivelled round to see the man in the England shirt standing very close behind her. He gripped her shoulder, pushed his mobile into her hand and said, 'Look at this then.'

Meghana looked at the tiny film that was playing out across the phone. Two men, one in a balaclava, the other with a keffiyeh scarf wrapped round his face, were stood looking straight to camera, while a third with his hands bound behind his back knelt on the ground between them. The man in the balaclava began speaking, very fast, in Arabic. Then he stopped, and the man in the keffiyeh scarf took over. Then he pulled out a knife and began to saw at the kneeling man's neck. The noise of his screaming rose, tinnily, from out of the phone, and a second later his blood covered most of the screen. Dave grabbed the phone out of Meghana's hand and threw it onto the floor, and then, with a surprising amount of force, he pushed the man in the England shirt away.

'Just fuck off okay mate? Now. Otherwise I'll get the landlord.'

'Ooo will you.' The man in the England shirt began to affect a clipped, upper-class accent. 'Will you get the landlord sir?'

The man in the England shirt started to stumble backwards, out of the room, pausing, just before he reached the exit, to pick up his phone, which was now lying in the doorway. He put it in his pocket, stood up and looking at Meghana said, 'You want to stop the war you black bitch? Then stop the fucking war.'

And then he disappeared.

01.09.2004

One of the lads couldn't find me on the list of new boys. I explained the Irish spelling and from then on I was Paddy. Considering Biffer, Thrombo and Billy the Stain also underwent a baptism of dirt this week, you could say I got off lightly. It's just that, well, I'm not sure it suits me ...

Antiphon

MEGHANA BUDANNAVAR ARRIVED BACK AT the house she shared with Matthew, another PhD student with whom she had nothing in common, shut the door and removed her shoes. She had never particularly liked living in Forest Fields, and had never been cool or edgy enough to find the used condoms and syringes that littered the alleyway behind the house anything other than depressing. But she appreciated how close it was, both to the university and to town, and it was cheap, so she put up with it. Plus, she could never decide on anywhere else that she wanted to live, considering everywhere else to be either too bourgeois or just as common.

Meghana padded up the stairs hoping Matthew wouldn't hear her, and then as soon as she was in her bedroom she burst into tears. She had been brought up to believe that the man in the England shirt, along with all those like him, was ignorant, unhappy and therefore to be pitied; and yet the memory of the two masked figures, or more specifically, the person they had slaughtered, was now splattered, irrevocably, across the insides of her skull.

She wiped her face and turned on her computer. Then she googled 'Jihadist beheading' and half a dozen video links immediately appeared. She let the mouse hover uncertainly over them, as if daring herself to confront the violence that each strip

of characters contained, before moving it back up to the navigation bar and typing out her usual 'www.blueyonder.co.uk'. She
signed into her account, and clicked on her only unread email,
which was from her father:

Dear Meghu,
    Just a quick note to wish you well and let you know that Auntie
Chanda has updated the blog. Also, your mother has been to see the
astrologer – who says that you will have some news for us soon.
    With love,
        Pappa X

Which translated as:

Dear Meghana who is still my baby,
    It is your duty to post a positive comment on Auntie Chanda's
blog – please do so as soon as possible to avoid bad feeling. Also,
your mother has been told, by forces larger than we are, that you will
soon become engaged.
    With love,
        Pappa X

With some love and much duty, Meghana then typed 'Go-
TeamBudannavar.blogspot.com' into the navigation bar, and a
picture of her cousin's graduation ceremony appeared. Then she
typed, 'Congratulations to Sandeep! Good to have another engineer in the family! With love, Meghu X' into the comments box
underneath it, and returned to the wide blue yonder:

Dear Pappa,
    I just had a quick look on Auntie's blog and saw Sandeep's
graduation pics. I left a comment saying congratulations. I don't
know what news Mum is expecting, but glad to know that whatever
it is it will be good – perhaps a distinction for my thesis?
    With love,
        Meghana X

52

Which translated as:

Dear Pappa who is inescapably my Pappa,
　I have done my duty as and when requested. Also I am not going to get engaged any time soon so please ask Mum to stop going on about it.
　With love (but grudgingly),
　　Meghana X

Meghana clicked on her Google search for 'Jihadist beheading' again, and 'GoTeamBudannavar.blogspot.com' again, and her emails again – each one of which made her feel a slightly different kind of queasy. Kathy had said that the Internet was the sea, whereas she herself had referred to it as an airport, but both of them had been wrong. The Internet, she now decided, was most definitely a web – and she was the fly it had caught.

She wiped her face again and turned off her computer. What she really wanted was a cup of tea the way her mother made it, which was very sweet with lemon, but she didn't want to go back downstairs until her eyes weren't red or until Matthew left the house. She looked round her depressingly tidy bedroom, taking in the books filled with case studies, and the files filled with photocopies of them, all of which she had arranged alphabetically on the shelves, and then the rail rammed with clothes, and the piles of shoes on the floor, none of which had ever suited her. She had always been seen as one of the good girls at her school, not a geek exactly, but definitely a high-achiever, and she'd also been reasonably well liked without ever fully understanding why. Maintaining order in the shape of excessive tidiness had always helped to quell the fear that she might one day be exposed as being neither particularly good nor particularly deserving of popularity, in much the same way that all the clothes, which she continued to buy compulsively, might somehow solve the question of who she really was.

'I need to put my right mind on the right things,' she said out loud, and as she did so she felt the weight not of her hair but of her locket.

Slowly, carefully, she opened it, removed the ishtalinga, and placed it in the centre of her palm. Slowly, carefully, she raised her hand until it was at eye level, and focused all her thoughts upon it, and then, only when everything inside of her was silent, did she begin to speak:

Kala beda, Kola beda
Husiya nudiyalu beda
Muniya beda
Anyarige asahya padabeda
Thanna bannisa beda
Idira haliyalu beda
Ide anthranga shuddi
Ide bahiranga shuddi
Ide namma koodala Sangamdevana
Olisuva pari

Which almost translated as:

Do not steal, do not kill
Do not lie
Do not get angry
Do not demean others
Do not glorify one's self
Do not hate others
This purifies the internal self
This purifies the external self
This is the way to get the love of Kudalasangama

Which would have translated as row upon row of curlicues had she been able to read, as well as speak Kannada, which she always did with her family, in Leicester.

Kala beda, Kola beda
Husiya nudiyalu beda—

54

'Meg, I'm going to the shop, do you want anything?' came Matthew's voice from the other side of the door.

Muniya beda
Anyarige asahya padabeda—

'I said I'm going to the shop do you want anything?' he repeated, and then, 'I SAID I'M GOING TO THE SHOP—'
'I'M FINE THANKS MATT!'
There was the sound of heavy footsteps and then the door slammed behind him, making the whole house shudder. A silence that wasn't just inside her filled up the rest of her depressingly tidy room. Slowly, carefully, Meghana lowered her hand and put the ishtalinga back inside her locket. Then she stood up and padded back downstairs. She put the kettle on and made herself a cup of tea and then, without thinking, she took out her mobile and called Dave's number.
'Hey Meg, are you alright?'
Straight away the man in the England shirt surged back into her brain, and after him the beheading and all the blood that, one way or another, had stained her. In the background she heard the door slam, and felt the whole house shudder, followed by the sound of Matthew trudging back upstairs.
'Yes of course. Of course,' she said quickly. 'I'm fine now. I don't know why I rang really.'
'Oh well, seeing as you did, are you doing anything Wednesday?'
'No. Why?'
'Well I was thinking that maybe we could, err, that maybe we could go for a drink ...?'

55

Confession and Absolution

KATARZYNA KWIATKOWSKA ATTEMPTED TO REARRANGE herself into a more comfortable position than the rather uncomfortable seats in the New College Media Hub allowed. Everything in the Media Hub, like everything everywhere, was becoming smaller and flatter, and generally being designed to take up less physical space, unlike the old monitor and accompanying hard drive that she had just managed to acquire free of charge as the result of this recent refurbishment, and which were now wedged between her knees for the rest of her session, until she could lug them onto the bus and then round to Margaret's, so that Margaret could email Eoin whenever she wanted and not have to rely on static-filled phone calls anymore.

'Okay so I'm going to give everyone ten more minutes to get organised and then we'll begin the presentations,' said Jackson, the Access to Media lecturer.

Katarzyna and the other students looked up at him for a second and then back down at their computer screens.

'Actually could we have twenty minutes?' said the boy beside her.

'Well the hand-in was officially one hour ago. So ten minutes is already kind of pushing it.'

'But the Media Hub was closed at the weekend,' said a girl whose attendance had averaged once a term so far. 'So really we all need an extra two days.'

'She's right,' said the boy. 'I mean we should all have extensions really because of exten – extenuat ...'

'Extenuating circumstances?'

'Yeah that's right.'

'Alright then. Twenty minutes.'

Jackson looked over at Katarzyna and sighed, and Katarzyna looked down at the monitor wedged between her knees. She knew that she was his favourite, in part because she was clever, but mainly because she always did her homework, and she knew too that both these things were embarrassing. Likewise, she knew that he would especially like her current project, 'St Barnabas Cathedral: The Architecture of Belief', because it sounded like something that Meg or Dave or another member of the bona fide middle classes might have written, even though it had actually not been written, but filmed, by her.

'So Kathy, I hear that you've made a documentary?' said Jackson.

Katarzyna nodded, mutely, at the old fat bits of computer by her feet, and then waited for him to go away. Then, as soon as he had wandered off, she clicked onto Astro Alerts, and then, as soon as Astro Alerts had flashed up on one of the new, flat screens, she clicked onto her horoscope, which was Cancer, which meant that she was loyal, caring, adaptable and responsive (or moody, clingy, self-pitying and self-absorbed, depending on your astrological compatibility):

Now is not the time to try to force any outcomes, but a time to meditate upon what is happening, and listen to your inner voice. You may be thinking about a recent personal experience or trying to understand the meaning of a present one. Something from the past is trying to re-enter your awareness.

Then she clicked onto Eoin's horoscope, which was Capricorn, which meant that he was responsible, disciplined, self-controlled and good at managing (or know-it-all, unforgiving, condescending and expecting the worst):

While the Full Moon calls attention to the need to make substantial changes, you are still trying to understand what needs to stay and what needs to go. Annoying and, possibly, worrying as these changes seem, they're an invitation to consider new options that, once you explore them, will ultimately prove rewarding.

And then she remembered that six whole weeks had now gone by since she had heard anything at all from Eoin, returned to her emails and clicked compose:

Dear Eoin,
I don't want to force the issue, but I don't understand what is happening. If I'm honest I'm not just annoyed, I'm also worried, and then I think that there must be a reason why you haven't been in touch . . .

And then she deleted it. She looked over towards the boy beside her. He was using a program called Photoshop, which enabled him to enlarge the breasts of an already well-endowed Page Three model. Then she turned to the girl on her left, who was looking at pictures of female celebrities, some of whom had been caught being overweight on holiday. Then she clicked onto another set of horoscopes, and then another until she eventually found one that said 'delays in communication will soon be coming to an end' . . .

'Okay, so we're going to begin now,' said Jackson.

'Can we have five more minutes?' said the boy beside her.

'No,' said Jackson, and then, 'Okay Tom, why don't we start with you?'

A boy at the back got up and began to fiddle with the overhead projector.

'So, err, yeah. So I've made a film about the differences between Forest fans and County fans.'

Jackson dimmed the lights and the first lot of amateur footage, in which Tom was standing in front of the Nottingham Forest Ground talking to groups of men in red-and-white shirts, lit up the back wall. The group watched as Tom asked each man questions such as, 'Why do you support Forest?' or 'Do you think that Forest are the best team in Nottingham?' and then listened to each man's answer, which was either 'Because they're the best team in Nottingham' or 'Yes'. Then someone else put the lights back on and Jackson said, 'Okay, so any questions?'

The whole room looked at the floor.

'Okay so Laura how about you?'

A girl got up and replaced Tom's film with a PowerPoint.

'So I've made an advertising campaign to publicise Lenny's – a restaurant in my area.'

She clicked onto the first slide, which showed pictures of both the interior and the exterior of Lenny's Sports Bar.

'I wanted to give it a really homely feel.'

She clicked onto the second slide, which showed the same pictures of Lenny's Sports Bar superimposed on a blue gingham background.

'So yeah that's it really.'

Someone else turned off the projector and Jackson said, 'Okay, so any questions?'

The room wriggled uncomfortably in their seats.

'Okay so Kathy, why don't you go next? I'm sure you've got something wonderful to show us.'

Katarzyna looked at Jackson and thought about how, if she were to discover that Eoin had died, it would be better than to discover that he had stopped loving her, because that way she could keep on loving him but without any shame. She thought that this might be because she was loyal, caring, adaptable and responsive, or because she was moody, clingy, self-pitying and self-absorbed, but that either way she loved him, and that love, and not Gothic Revivalism, was the architecture of belief – and then she remembered that delays in communication would soon be coming to an end . . .

'Kathy?' said Jackson.

'Err, I'm not sure that my file's compatible with the system. I think I'll have to send it to you afterwards.'

Because love, and not Gothic Revivalism, was the architecture of belief.

'Okay, but I have to say that I'm a little disappointed.'

Katarzyna nodded at the floor and pulled her baseball cap down so that it hid her face with shadow; and then she thought about how, even at twenty-three years of age, she was still stuck, either in prison or in purgatory, or at a school called English Martyrs.

Prayers of the Faithful

MARGARET O'SHEA PRESSED A RAG that had once been a pair of underpants against the top of the Brasso bottle and then turned it upside down, before handing it to Blessings, who did exactly the same. Then the two women sat in silence for some time, earnestly polishing the candlesticks, not all of which were used or needed, until the only thing that registered about the small church hall was the smell of petrol and ammonia. Margaret watched as Blessings worked her rag into a particularly intricate section of candlestick, and then, very cautiously, said, 'Perhaps next month you could *assist* me with the flowers.'

Blessings bowed her head. 'That is very kind of you Margaret.'

'And we have been getting some beautiful blooms lately. You know Danny's daughter? Well she's a florist see, and that means that—'

'Danny is not a good man,' said Blessings.

Margaret picked up her rag again but then put it down and twisted the sleeve of her blouse uncertainly. She knew that Blessings' comment must have had something to do with Danny's not shaking hands – but how on earth did she know about it? Father Jonathan generally preferred to make oblique comments that involved quotations from the gospel rather than saying anything to anyone directly, which meant that it must have been one of the new black families from Rwanda, gossiping ...

61

'Danny has had a hard life,' Margaret said carefully, 'before he moved here you see, he lived in Rathcoole, and when you grow up in a place like that you get, well, you get scared to trust those who aren't your own. You—'

But then she stopped, not wanting to say any more, because more meant the beatings, doled out on Orange Day. Or the 'missing' votes. Or, of course, what had happened to her own dear Steven ... And then she thought about all of the other collections, besides those at St Flannan's. The ones where they'd never said where the money was going, only that there were people, just like them, who were prepared to die for justice ...

'Do you know Albertina?' said Blessings.

'The Rwandan lady?' said Margaret, because all of the Rwandan ladies had French-sounding names.

'Albertina is Tutsi, and Didier, her husband, he was Hutu.'

Margaret nodded, although she didn't understand quite what this meant, and then waited patiently for Blessings to explain.

'When Albertina and Didier went to mass Albertina would take their daughters and walk one way, and Didier would take their sons and walk the other. That way, if anyone attacked them, then half their family would survive. But Didier did not survive. Nor did Albertina's father, nor her brothers. Her brothers were killed in front of her. Some with a gun and some with a machete.'

'But ... but ... oh dear,' said Margaret – because what else could she say?

'But Albertina is still a Christian. And when she says "peace be with you" she still holds out her hand.'

A horrible silence followed, during which all Margaret could do was press a rag that had once been a pair of underpants against the top of the Brasso bottle and then turn it upside down. She felt herself filling up with rage lest this other, foreign woman's suffering might somehow diminish her and Danny and Padraig and Sinead's own, or that the death of a husband and a daughter might no longer be considered enough, when it was enough, enough to break you even – and then, just as suddenly she felt ashamed and sorry for Albertina.

62

'Well I'm glad that Albertina is safe now,' Margaret said eventually, and then, because she was desperate for something else to get away from it, she continued, 'I don't know much about Rwanda, but for some reason I've always pictured mountains.'

'It is the mountains that Albertina misses most. It is too dangerous for her to go back now, but one day when she has saved enough money she will visit Uganda and look at them from there.'

'And have you been to Rwanda, Blessings?'

'No, I have never been.'

'Or Uganda perhaps?'

'No. I am from Malawi.'

'Yes I know that,' said Margaret, almost irritably, 'but I thought that you might have visited.'

Blessings picked up the Brasso bottle again, but in a way that was somehow more assertive than before.

'And have you ever visited Paris?'

'No I haven't,' said Margaret, very firmly, and then, 'Now, I think that we could both do with a cup of tea don't you?'

She stood up and removed her hearing aid, putting it in her pocket. But by the time she reached the kitchen her annoyance had already faded. Instead she thought about how funny it was that all of the African ladies, even the ones with English names, or at any rate English words, thought non-stop about all things French – almost as if it were the 1950s – and then the kettle boiled, and she put the tea things on a tray and shuffled back out into the hall.

'I'm sorry but there don't seem to be any biscuits,' said Margaret.

But Blessings only laughed and patted her small, round stomach. 'You must not worry about biscuits Margaret. I eat too many sweet things as it is.'

'Oh no, no Blessings not at all. You're a fine, fine figure of a woman so you are.'

Margaret put down the tray and watched as Blessings picked up the milk and sniffed it, even though she didn't need to sniff it because Margaret had bought it fresh that morning, and then put it back again untouched. Without sniffing it, Margaret picked it up and added a drop to her own tea. 'I suppose that things are very different in Malawi?' she said cautiously.

'Malawi is a very poor country. There are no prospects.'

'No prospects?'

'The educational system is not very good, and there aren't many jobs. Here I have a place on Access to Business Studies. If I pass, then I will become a professional person.'

'At New College? That's where Eoin's fiancée goes.'

Blessings put a lump of sugar in her tea without milk, while Margaret took another sip from her off-white cup.

'And how is your grandson, Margaret?'

'Oh he's grand, he's grand. Or at least I hope he is. I mean I think – I hope, that he'll be calling me on Sunday.'

Thanksgiving

STANISŁAW KWIATKOWSKI WALKED UP PAST the Cathedral and turned left into the Park Estate. Although most of the larger houses had now been divided up into flats, traces remained of a once affluent past. There were still Victorian gas lamps, signs saying 'Servants' Entrance' attached to the wrought-iron gates and – a particularly strange affectation – blue instead of yellow lines drawn around the edges of the streets. He walked up to one of the most elegant houses and placed his fat, pink finger confidently on the buzzer.

'Stańko!' came a voice that sounded like Stanisław's voice, and a second later Józek Woźniak appeared.

'Józek!' And the two men embraced, slapping each other on the shoulders.

Having arrived in England within a month of each other had been all that it had taken to cement a lifelong friendship between these two disparate and displaced people. Both men hated the old country in equal measure, and both felt an odd, almost painful affection for their new one – a combination that kept them even warmer than the the fog of alcohol through which they tended to discuss it. A moment or so passed before the men let go of each other and went inside, and Stanisław made himself comfortable in the large leather armchair by the window. Józek poured two glasses of vodka, handed one to Stanisław and then in Polish said,

'So how is Katarzyna? I trust that getting married won't keep her from her studies?'

Stanisław downed his vodka, then took a cigarette from the packet that was lying on the table and lit it.

'It's not the idea of her getting married, or even dropping out of college that worries me,' he said at last, and also in Polish, 'it's more her attitude generally. I mean this lad that she thinks she's in love with, this Eoin. He's a soldier for Christ's sake. He's in the army.'

Józek also reached for a cigarette, while at the same time stroking his moustache. With practised weariness he said, 'You know I never joined the party. It would have fast-tracked my career no doubt – even at the university these things didn't go unnoticed – but how could I have looked my friends, my family in the eye?'

'Exactly Józek. Exactly. Kasia, even Iwona, sometimes, she tells me that it's different now. But how is it different? It's different for us because we're living in a rich country, but is it any different for those who aren't?'

Józek nodded and Stanisław exhaled, thinking as he did so of the two department stores that, during his life in Gdańsk, were the only two places that had sold this type of cigarettes, and then later, when things got even worse, were the only two that stocked even basic things like toilet paper – except that no one other than the sailors could afford to shop there, because all they took was US dollars. After communism had ended, the situation had become even worse, due to the lack of infrastructure. Suddenly, there were department stores filled with Western goods aplenty, each and every one of which took zloty – and yet the only difference, as far as Stanisław could see, was that his former countrymen could then stare at things they couldn't afford rather than shelves and shelves of nothing . . .

'But this soldier, this Eoin, he must have a reason for joining up surely?' said Józek, refilling both their glasses.

Stanisław downed another shot, stubbed out his first cigarette and lit a second.

'But that's just it, he doesn't. He just seems to have ended up there, in the same way he might have ended up being an accountant, and Kasia, she seems to think that's normal. And yet she's such a beautiful girl ... and clever too,' he continued, as Józek began to pick, ruefully, at the label on the vodka bottle. 'She could have anything, anything she wanted but something inside her—'

'Guilt?'

'I don't know. Maybe. But whatever it is it just won't allow her to reach for it. Or even to just enjoy herself.'

A contemplative silence followed, during which he and Józek leaned back in their chairs. The room had now filled up with an acrid, stale odour that made Stanisław feel pleasantly at home, even though at his actual home his wife had forbidden smoking. He reminded himself of how, so long as he walked back afterwards, the fresh air would get rid of the worst of it, while the rest could be blamed on a bonfire at one of the nearby allotments – a not unusual occurrence at this time of year ...

'Sometimes it is easier for the person who is oppressed to imagine being happy,' Józek said thoughtfully, 'than for the person who is supposed to be free. You remember the Pope's visit, Stańko? You remember seventy-nine?'

Stanisław exhaled and nodded.

'Of course I remember.'

'Then you must also remember when he left?'

And again Stanisław remembered.

'Well, we didn't have a television Stańko, and neither did many of our friends, but one of our neighbours did, and so we all crowded into their house to watch. Then, as I saw the plane take off I was overcome with panic. It weighed on my chest like a heavy stone – the thought that the one man who could help us was leaving and that we were alone in this hell once more. Without thinking, I got up, pushed through everybody and ran outside. And then I stood there, in the middle of the street, squinting into the sun – except nothing. Not one single plane flew over—'

'I know but—'

'But then, when I looked around me I saw that the street was full. And I realised that everybody else had done exactly what I had done, and run outside to look for the plane – and I knew then that we were many, and that we would rise up together. And I knew then that a great change was coming. And at that moment I felt completely free, for the first, perhaps the only time in my life, because at that moment I felt as if something new was possible.'

Stanisław nodded, and picked up his glass. He looked at the window, which was patent black, because neither he nor Józek had bothered to draw the curtains, although it still wasn't really dark or cold, or dark or cold like Gdańsk. And then he took another drag and said, 'It's a moving story Józek, but I am not like you, or my daughter for that matter. Captive or free I have no imagination. My feelings result from my experiences, as I experience them, here and now. Here I can enjoy milk chocolate and oranges every day of the week, and not just at Christmas. And that means that I do not need, nor want, to hope – although of course I still remember.'

Blessing, Dismissal

DR DAVID GOLDSTEIN WALKED UP to the cathedral at the top of Derby Road, deposited the remainder of his nicotine gum on the wall in front of it, and walked self-consciously inside. Having finally decided to test the philosophy of the Kaosphere he was now obliged to do something that, in spite of his extensive studies in the area, he had never attempted to do before, and experience some of the migrant communities' religions first hand. Indeed all of his prior knowledge, he now realised, had been limited, primarily, to focus groups, in which he had plied the participants (or 'Case Study One: The Polish Community in Sneinton' and 'Case Study Two: The Irish Community in The Meadows') with weak squash, strong tea and cheap biscuits, and then asked them to answer a series of questions:

On a scale of one to ten, one meaning strongly disagree and ten meaning strongly agree, please record your responses to the following statements:

1: My religious affiliations are an important part of my identity.
2: My religious practices help me to preserve my culture.
3: My religious beliefs inform my political beliefs.

He would then switch on the recording equipment that he had borrowed from the geography department, and ask each member of the group not only to explain the reasons for their responses, but also to try to elicit the key words and phrases that each one of these questions had evoked – all of which would then be record-ed on a flipchart pad while people strongly agreed, or disagreed, with the aforementioned words or phrases, or else doodled on their forms.

Now, however, David pushed all thoughts of his notes to one side, and instead looked up at the high vaulted ceiling and then down at the criss-crossing tiles on the floor, none of which ap-peared to have any relation to his research despite the fact that both the Polish Community in Sneinton and the Irish Commu-nity in The Meadows frequented, and worshiped in, the space. He knew, from the book that Kathy had lent him, that most of the Cathedral was built in the plain Gothic style, but he could already see something up ahead that belonged to the more for-eign, and therefore decorative variety. Instinctively he made his way towards this other, semi-separate room. Votive candles half lit the space and a large gold object, reminiscent of a Fabergé egg, wrapped in miniature velvet curtains was placed, centre stage, upon the altar. He was just about to kneel down in front of it, and attempt to lose himself in the incense and candle flicker, when an old lady, not dissimilar to the one he had seen with Stan and Kathy, tapped him on the shoulder and ushered him outside. He watched as she pulled what looked like a child's safety gate across the entrance and then, before he could even ask her what the problem was, she locked it.

'Are you new?' she whispered, and David nodded.

The old lady nodded back and then pressed a hymnbook into his hands before shuffling him into a pew right at the front of the church. David waited and, as soon as she was out of sight, stood up, eager to move nearer to the back. Yet before he could do so the rest of the congregation rose around him, singing a hymn which, not being of the vague and flowery kind he had sung at school, he was unable to join in with. As the service progressed, he watched out for when those on either side of him stood or knelt or sat, and then followed suit a few seconds after. He felt a little sad to realise that the drama and sorrow (or opulence and poverty) that he had anticipated was lacking, and that the mass consisted, by and large, of ordinary, English people ...

We believe in one God,
The Father, the Almighty,
Maker of heaven and earth,
Of all that is seen and unseen.
We believe ...

Suddenly David realised that those on either side of him had stood up again, and again he stumbled after them. We believe. We believe. We believe, they said. And each time a chain of events, real or imagined, followed in a waterfall of not quite history. He thought that it was beautiful – the chanting and the standing all at once, or nearly all at once, and nearly all together, but all together believing; and then he thought of how if only he too had known the words then he too would have said and tried to mean them.

David stood and sat and knelt, and then he took communion and said 'Amen', which he knew had come from ancient Aramaic, via ancient Greek, via ancient Latin. He tried again to sing the hymns he didn't know, and then sat down again and stood up again until everything had ended. He waited until the last of the altar boys had walked back down the aisle and the sound of the organ had ceased, and then he too genuflected, and made the sign of the cross, going up and down and side to side across his forehead, stomach and chest ...

'Are you new?' said the priest, who was standing by the door with what could have been the same old lady.

'Yes,' said David, taking hold of the priest's outstretched hand and almost dropping his hymnbook in the process. 'And I've travelled quite some way to get here.'

'Oh? Well I hope that we'll be seeing more of you?'

David tried to smile, then handed his hymnbook over, before walking back outside and into the fresh new darkness. As he scrutinised the other parishioners filing out alongside him, he thought once more about St Flannan's, and then the Polish Mission, and then the Russian Orthodox Church, where there was sure to be not only golden eggs aplenty but also patriarchs, whose bearded appearance resembled the Warhammer dwarves ... But then, just as he turned towards the bus stop, he ran directly into Stan.

'Why you here Dave?' he said.

'Oh here?' And suddenly David felt embarrassed. 'Well I-I thought I'd, err, see what all the, err, fuss was about and, err ...'

An old copy of *The Economist* fluttered into the gutter, the cover of which momentarily took up both of their attention. It depicted a hooded man standing on top of a box with electric wires attached to his hands. The magazine must have been at least six months old, and David had bought and read a copy of it at the time, but it was still an image that had the power to shock and to keep on shocking and accordingly he kept on staring at it, until Stan bent down and scrunched it up into a dirty, unintelligible ball of paper.

'Bad business,' said Stan, pushing the ball into a nearby bin, and then, 'But you have the Jew's name yes?'

'Well, I mean, yes, my dad is. Was. Still is I suppose. But my mother isn't and it's, err, it's passed down on your mother's side you see so, err ...'

'You lose people in Holocaust?'

'Well I suppose so, somewhere along the way. I mean everyone has though, if you go far enough back, I, err, I mean ...'

'No not everyone Dave. Jews.'

David popped out another piece of nicotine gum, partly because the smell of Stan reminded him that he too wanted a cigarette and partly because it had now become his default mechanism whenever he couldn't think of anything suitable to say. Stan watched him for a moment, then slapped his shoulder, as always a little too hard, before setting off back down Derby Road. After a few seconds he stopped, turned round and shouted, 'You know the word you looking for?'

David put the fresh piece of gum in his mouth and shook his head, while Stanisław flung out his sweaty arms and laughed. 'Solidarność, Dave. Solidarność!'

The Rite of the Discordiant Die

THIS RITE PROVIDES A METHODOLOGY through which to disorder established belief systems based upon the Principia Discordia, or Law of Fives, in which it is stated that all things are directly or indirectly appropriate to five: the use of humour; randomness; and a pre-existing feedback survey. It is intended to function as a test of the magician's ability to perform any version of any truth at a given point in time.

STATEMENT OF INTENT:
It is my will that I will believe what I believe for as long as I believe it.

RITE:
1. Open with the Unequal Opportunities Rite.
2. Select five dice, all of which should be grey (i.e. an achromatic colour) so as to emphasise bureaucracy.
3. Cast the first die, using the following formula: 1 = Monotheism, 2 = Polytheism, 3 = Atheism, 4 = Nihilism, 5 = Superstition. Remember, if you appear to have cast a six (i.e. a number that is neither below nor divisible by five), then you have created an illusion, and should therefore re-cast until the temporary and subjective truth that you want to appear, appears.
4. Say the Statement of Intent.

5. Cast the second die, equating odd numbers with inhibitory gnosis (yoga, meditation, trance work and so on), and even numbers with excitatory gnosis (dancing, chanting, sex, etc.).
6. Repeat the Statement of Intent.
7. Cast the third die, using the following formula: 1 = a minute, 2 = an hour, 3 = a day, 4 = a week, 5 = a month.
8. Repeat the Statement of Intent.
9. Cast the fourth and fifth dice and then add their scores together, equating the lower scores with varying levels of belief, the higher scores with varying levels of disbelief and five with neither belief nor disbelief, which being five is sacred (N.B. while there is a strong chance that a score that is neither below nor divisible by five may now occur, remember that truth, like illusion, is temporary, and accordingly the die need not be re-cast on this, different occasion).
10. Using the results of the previous castings formulate a sentence that summarises the type, method, length and strength of your randomly generated belief system (e.g. 'I strongly believe in the practice of nihilistic dancing for one week').
11. Repeat the Statement of Intent.
12. Perform your sentence for as long as your sentence requires.
13. Banish, very suddenly, by laughing, stopping abruptly, and then saying, 'Well I mean it's all very well saying that now, but at the time it made sense.'

Exodus

DR DAVID GOLDSTEIN HEADED STRAIGHT for the little half cellar in which his parents kept wine, and then selected a bottle of Burgundy, with which he intended either to celebrate or to commiserate – he was still not entirely sure which word to use – his second attempt to test the Kaosphere theorem. He had just returned from the synagogue, an experience that had left him feeling utterly disorientated, not just because the service had been difficult to understand, but also because it had been difficult to find out about, which in turn meant that it had been difficult to prepare for, all of which had, once again, made him feel like an outsider – although it wasn't as if he hadn't tried. In fact, he had left numerous messages prior to his visit, but neither the liberal nor the orthodox rabbi had answered; and yet when he had eventually brought this up with his father the old man had merely laughed and said well what did he expect – the Jews were a closed shop.

Eventually David had had no choice but to resort to Wikipedia, or more specifically the page entitled Shabbat, after which he had asked his mother to light a candle because one of the hyperlinks had told him that on Friday night the women lit candles. And then he had attempted to bake a loaf of bread because another hyperlink had told him that on Friday night the women baked bread – only his mother had refused to help out with that one.

And then on Saturday morning he had put on his suit, which was the same suit that he had had since sixth form but which was still too big on the shoulders, and headed off into town where Google Earth had shown him a picture of a former Wesleyan chapel now repurposed as a synagogue.

Yet things had gone well upon arrival, in the sense that everything that he had initially encountered had tallied with what the Internet had told him. A basket of kippahs was set out on a table in the entrance, and likewise a rack of prayer shawls, so that David, like all of the other men milling round him, had been able to put on one of each, and then say the following words:

'Barukh ata Adonai Eloheynu Melekh ha'olam, asher kidshanu b'mitz-votav l'hitatef ba'tzitzit.'

Which he had first heard via Rabbi Emma, via Williamsburg via YouTube, before typing it into Babelfish, which had more or less translated it as:

'Blessed are you God, sovereign of the universe who has sanctified us with the commandments and commanded us to wrap ourselves in cotton fringes knotted in such a way as to indicate the oneness of God.'

Which would have translated as row upon row of angular, back-to-front letters that ran from right to left had he been able to read, instead of merely analyse, Hebrew, the language of his father's past.

Once inside the sanctuary things had felt different, however. More mysterious, which he had instinctively equated with being more spiritual. He noticed that the space was segregated, and that all the women were sitting with covered heads in the gallery above, and also that there was a cupboard containing objects that, upon first glance, were not dissimilar to the Fabergé egg up at the Cathedral, although these, he discovered, contained not bread, or wafers, or possibly even God, but scrolls. When the cupboard was open everybody stood up, and when it was closed everybody sat down, which, in this one and possibly only respect made the service easier to follow. In the beginning he watched the cupboard, but then as time went on he began to look around him, and to notice the other scrolls, or rather the other representations of them. These were carved out of white marble, and then mounted on the surrounding walls, where the first fragments of text, written not in Assyrian script but incised Roman capitals, read:

In everlasting remembrance
Of the sons of this congregation
Who fell in the Great War 1914–1918

This inscription was followed by a list of 124 names, including a Gold, a Goldman and even a Goodman (but no Goldstein), as well as three men, presumably brothers, who all shared the surname Lazarus. David had expected a Holocaust memorial, not a war memorial, and the thought that these men had given their lives for England, as much as Israel, which at that time was still Palestine, meaning both a memory and a dream, was one that he found strangely moving. A profound sense of time simultaneously passing and standing still, of himself as both a passive and an active force within it, suddenly overcame him, and then just as suddenly he realised that the service, if it could be called a service, had ended . . .

David poured himself a very large glass of the Burgundy, sat down at the kitchen table, and cut himself a slice of bread that, due to what he had now chosen to view as his mother's disinterest, had not risen. He took a sip of wine, while contemplating whether or not the addition of marmalade could be considered in any way sacrilegious, when his father wandered in, in search of *The Times*.

'Isn't it a little early for that?' he asked.

'It's kiddush.'

David raised his glass in the same way that he might have done had he been saying 'cheers', while his father shook his head and laughed.

'That's not kiddush.'

'It's not?'

'It's definitely not.'

'Then show me.'

There was an awkward pause, and then his father moved the bottle and glass out of the way. He covered the bread with a tea towel, and began to recite something in what David now recognised as Hebrew, but which, as far as he could remember, had not shown up on any of the Wikipedia pages. When he had finished he looked at David, who instinctively said 'Amen', and then he bowed his head, or maybe nodded. Then he went over to one of the cupboards and took out a cup and saucer, and began to pour in the wine until it ran over the top of the cup.

'Watch out!' said David.

'HaShem's blessing overflows into our lives.' His father tipped a little of his cup back into David's glass, and then chinked his against it. 'Kiddish David.'

'Oh, err, yeah. Cheers.'

As David resumed drinking his Burgundy, he thought once more of his focus groups, and wondered what, if he himself were to attend one not as an observer but as a participant, his own answers would be now:

1: My religious affiliations are an important part of my identity – five.

2: My religious practices help me to preserve my culture – five.

3: My religious beliefs inform my political beliefs – five.

Five, five, five, thought David, which meant that he neither agreed nor disagreed with any of the statements that he had written for other people to answer, which meant that, had he been forced to include his own responses each one of them would have been as good as void. He took another sip of Burgundy, and then another, savouring the red, earthy taste and then, thinking of this and little else, he allowed the glass to slip from his hands, and overflowed onto the table.

Exodus

MARGARET O'SHEA STOPPED, STOOPED AND rubbed her knees,
which as always ached. Then, when she stood up again, the sudden rush of blood to the head made her dizzy. She held out one
arm, palm flat against the wall, and waited until the feeling had
passed, and then, when she was just about right again, she carried
on with the cleaning. She dusted each of the ornaments, pausing only when she reached those on the mantelpiece. Then she
picked up a pen and made a cross on the calendar, which meant
that every square of October was now filled. As she looked at it
she thought about the ways in which the days, which had turned
into weeks, which had turned into months, were slowly filling up
and drifting by while the roses, like the little blue figure in front
of them, remained exactly the same as before.

Margaret sat down on the edge of the settee and took out her
rosary. She had said all four sets of all five mysteries, which added
up to twenty mysteries each day, each day that Eoin had been
away so far, which meant that she would have said 3,650 mysteries by the time he returned. Today she began, as always, with
the Joyful Mysteries, which meant that she began by making the
sign of the cross and saying the Apostles Creed; and then an Our
Father; and then three Hail Marys; and that then she announced
the First Mystery (which in this case was The Annunciation).
Then she said another Our Father; and then she said another

ten Hail Marys (while also trying to think about The Annunciation); and then she said the words 'Glory be to the Father . . .' In an attempt to further prolong the experience Margaret had recently taken to also inserting an extra prayer, as requested by the Blessed Virgin at Fatima; and then afterwards, if there was still time, she put in a quick Hail Holy Queen. And then, more often than not, she went back to the cleaning.

Today, however, Margaret not only put her rosary back in her pocket, but also her duster, before shuffling all the way upstairs to what was still Eoin's room, in which Kathy had installed her new computer; and which now meant that, even though Eoin wasn't able to ring or write to her as often as he would have liked, she could still write to him and he would still get it – instantly.

Margaret sat down and turned on the computer which, as if by magic, Kathy had linked up to the even more magical, or possibly devilish, Internet, and then she did as Kathy had done and typed 'www.gmail.com' into the navigation bar. Next she entered the email address that Kathy had set up for her, which was 'margaretoshea1929@gmail.com', into the little box beneath it, followed by the password that she had chosen for herself, which was '12345', and then she began to compose her first email:

Dear Eoin,
I hope that you are keeping well and making the most of the sunny weather. Kathy tells me that you are travelling to another camp – will it be beside the sea again, like Basra, or will it be in the desert, or even in the mountains? Will they let you take your dog with you, or does he have to stay back at the base? I could knit a coat for him if you'd like. Danny, Padraig and Sinead have all asked to be remembered to you, and next week Father Jonathan will say a mass for your safe return.
Please take care,
Nana X

Which translated as:

Dear Eoin,

My knees ache, my head aches, my heart aches, and regardless of whether or not I wear my hearing aid the whole world sounds like static.

You are all I have left,

Nana X

Margaret blinked, pressed her lips together and pressed 'send', making sure that what was meant to go out went out, and what was meant to stay in stayed in, even if that meant that what little was left of her was now set all atremble. Then she bowed her head and said another Hail Holy Queen, her voice breaking, only very slightly, as she neared the end: '. . . And after this our exile, show unto us the blessed fruit of thy womb, Jesus, Oh merciful, Oh loving, Oh sweet Virgin Mary! Amen.'

Amen – which she did not know had come from ancient Aramaic, via ancient Greek, via ancient Latin to England to Ireland and back again, but which she still translated as 'so be it'. Oh merciful, Oh loving, Oh sweet Virgin Mary, who is also the Holy Mother, the Holy Virgin, Our Lady of Sorrows, Grace, Light, Mercy, etc., after this, our exile . . .

'So be it,' said Margaret, out loud, and then turned off the computer.

She stood up again, and the sudden rush of blood to the head made her dizzy. She held out one arm, palm flat against the wall, and waited until the feeling had passed, and then, when she was just about right again, she shuffled back down the stairs and carried on with the cleaning. The clock on the wall was still ticking. There were still thirty-one crosses hanging over the little blue figure, and also a garden of roses; just as there were still November and December, waiting behind them, although no January or February, which, when they came, would bring other flowers . . .

The clock continued ticking while Margaret went over to the cupboard underneath the stairs and removed the hoover, and then removed the carpet brush from the extension tube so that she could get into all the cracks. It carried on ticking as the noise of the machine whirred above it, and she began to crawl around the little patterned room sucking up the nonexistent dirt. It carried on ticking when she stopped and rubbed her knees again, which now ached even more than usual, and then when she stood up again, the sudden rush of blood to the head made her dizzy. Again. And again she held out one arm, palm flat against the wall, and waited until the feeling had passed, and then, when she was just about right again, the clock's big and small hands jolted into the middle of the day.

Margaret sat down on the edge of the settee and began to say The Angelus, which she now said, as well as all four sets of all five mysteries, interspersed with the extra prayer requested by the Blessed Virgin at Fatima, and numerous Hail Holy Queens, at twelve o'clock and six o'clock each day.

'Amen,' said Margaret, again, and as she stood up the sudden rush of blood to the head made her dizzy.

She took out her hearing aid but could still hear the clock, which was still ticking – slightly faster than a heartbeat and far too fast for any more prayers, and then she decided that she would make herself a cup of tea and maybe even have a biscuit. And then she would carry on with the cleaning.

Leviticus

STANISŁAW KWIATKOWSKI LIFTED THE LID on the large iron casserole dish and inhaled the smell of golonka, which was Polish for pork knuckle. He could see that the meat was nearly ready, and that when his wife came to serve it, it would fall away, loose and tender from the bone, and ah yes, he thought, in a way that for him was almost dreamily, the one, the only thing worth missing about Poland is the food ...

'Stańko! You'll ruin it if you keep on peeking,' said Iwona, in Polish.

She slapped him sharply on the arm, and in response Stanisław replaced the lid and turned instead towards the fridge.

'And it's too early for a beer.'

'It's never too early for a beer.'

'That's debatable.' Iwona leaned in and sniffed his tee-shirt. 'And you need to change your clothes.'

Stanisław raised his eyebrows, but his wife was too absorbed in the golonka to notice. Then he ambled slowly up the stairs. He peeled off his bright yellow, 'In Case of Emergency Break *Dance*' tee-shirt and dumped it in the dirty laundry basket, splashed some water under his arms, and selected another bright green one that read 'I'm with Stupid', next to an arrow.

He went back down into the kitchen and kissed Iwona on the cheek.

'Better? Acceptable?'

'Acceptable. Just.'

Iwona picked up the casserole dish and carried it into the front room, along with the plates that had been warming in the oven. She was just about to sit down next to Stanisław when, as if thinking better of it, she moved her seat slightly to the left, so that the arrow on his tee-shirt now pointed to the casserole dish and not to her.

'I'm not stupid.'

'I wouldn't have married you if you were stupid,' said Stanisław, taking his first mouthful of golonka, 'or if you couldn't cook.'

'Or sew, or play the accordion. I'm like a Polish geisha.'

Stanisław looked at his blonde, well-kept wife, who kept him well also, and laughed with amusement and pleasure. He tore a piece of bread from the loaf in the middle of the table and cut a piece of butter that was thicker than a thick piece of cheese. He thought about how England was not only his home but the home that he and Iwona had made for each other, and yet he knew that if he said, 'England is my home', or even 'England is the place where my wife and I have lived all our adult lives', let alone tried to explain that his daughter spoke Polish with an English accent and English with a Nottingham accent to anyone other than another immigrant then they would look at him like he was raving . . .

He sopped up what remained of the golonka with the bread, while pushing what remained of the golonka-soaked potatoes into his mouth. Then he looked up at the picture of Pope John Paul II and said, 'I'm worried about Kasia.'

Iwona tutted and scraped the remnants of her dinner back into the casserole dish. 'You're always worried about Kasia. But she is already five years older than I was when we got married.'

'I know. I was just thinking that.'

Iwona tutted again and began to stack their empty plates together. 'Well then. She is old enough to make her own decisions. I certainly was.'

'You were yes. You knew how to fight for what you wanted. But Kasia . . .' Again he looked at the picture, thinking firstly of Eoin, and then of the photograph on the cover of *The Economist*. 'I just don't want her to be disappointed, that's all.'

Iwona piled the plates on top of the casserole dish and went back into the kitchen, returning a few minutes later with two cups of very strong tea. She handed one to Stanisław and said, 'I like Eoin. I think that he and Kasia make a nice couple.'

Stanisław took his cup and repositioned himself on the settee. 'I don't dislike Eoin.'

'Don't you?'

'I neither like nor dislike him.' And then, as if this unconscious reference to Dave's migrant scoring system had somehow pushed the memory of him to the forefront of Stanisław's mind, 'I like Dave.'

'Dave?'

'The guy who took her for a beer.'

'But she hardly knows him!'

'But I hardly knew you. I just knew that I loved you and that was enough.'

'Oh Stańko, really.' Iwona slapped his arm again and then removed the tissue paper parcel, upon which Stanisław had inadvertently placed his cup of tea. 'I think that was a little different.'

'Different how?'

'A different country. In many ways.'

Stanisław looked at her and sighed. The tissue paper parcel, he now realised, contained two yards of Koniaków lace. It was only a matter of time before the date would be set and the church would be booked, and then the whole world as he knew it, the whole tiny world in which he was now obliged, against his better judgement, to form some sense of hope, would have changed forever.

'But Dave lives in West Bridgford,' he said, despondently.

'And we live in Sneinton. And your Kasia's not such an innocent as you like to think, just as Eoin's not so worldly wise.'

'I never said that Eoin was wise.'

'And I say he's not stupid.'

Her eye moved back to Stanisław's tee-shirt and, remembering the arrow, she got up and sat back down on the other side of the settee.

'You know that Józek never joined the party?' Stanisław continued.

'And nor did I if you remember rightly?'

'Of course I remember. But what about all the people we knew who did? Who said that it didn't matter because they were still the same person. But they weren't the same person. Even if the party itself didn't change them, everybody else's reaction to it did. And it made them become them, while we stayed us. And then they had to act like them, and then they hated us. When we were in Poland—'

'I can hardly remember Poland,' said Iwona, still in Polish. 'Or why I didn't join the party. Or even what the party means. Now do you want another cup of tea?'

'No, you don't want to remember Poland, which is different,' said Stanisław, glaring at the tissue paper. 'And what I would like is a beer.'

Numbers

MEGHANA BUDANNAVAR SCANNED THE EVENING Post Classifieds office until she located Kathy, who looked up from behind her computer screen and pointed at the Stop the War Coalition badge, which was pinned to her sweatshirt collar. She raised her own hand to wave back, only before she had the chance to do so Judy took hold of her arm.

'Oh, I'm okay thanks,' said Meghana, noticing the tartan tin that Judy was carrying, 'I had a sandwich on the way.'

For a moment Judy looked puzzled, and then, as if seeing the tin for the first time, laughed.

'Oh no, not that. Something even better.'

'Really?'

Meghana tried not to sound too incredulous. Although she had little doubt that there were indeed better things available than Judy's souvenir shortbreads, she couldn't help but think it unlikely that they were to be found in the Free Ads section.

'Yes. I've had you moved to Family Announcements.'

'Well that's very kind of you but, err ...'

'Now don't start being all silly and polite about it.' Judy gave her arm a gentle squeeze. 'We all do what we can.'

Meghana looked back over at Kathy and scowled and shrugged her shoulders, before then sitting down beside Aaeesha, who continued to flick through *Heat*. Then she put her headset on and typed 'www.blueyonder.co.uk' into the navigation bar – except that the little green light on the switchboard lit up straight away. Reluctantly she clicked onto the Family Announcements screen, and pressed 'answer'.

'Hello, Evening Post Family Announcements. Meg speaking how can I help you?'

'Alright duck. I want to have a bereavement printed.'

Meghana began to type into one of the Family Announcements boxes.

'And could I have the name of the deceased?'

'Iris.'

'And could you tell me Iris's surname?'

'Bradley.'

'Okay, I'm just going to read that back to you using the phonetic alphabet to check that I've got the correct spelling. That's Iris – India, Romeo, India, Sierra – Bradley – Bravo, Romeo, Alpha, Delta, Lima, Echo, Yankee. Is that right?'

'What's a lima?' said the voice on the other end, 'Is it a llama?'

'It's the capital of Peru. Is that the correct spelling?'

'Yes duck.'

'And what message would you like to leave for Iris?'

'Oh right, hang on . . .' The noise of heavy breathing now filled up both of Meghana's ears. 'Just give me a minute, okay?'

'Take your time.'

Meghana broke off a piece of the shortbread.

'Err, okay duck, I've found my piece of paper, let me read it out to you – much-loved sister-in-law and favourite Auntie who always made us smile. A genuine woman who we will always love and remember. Goodnight Iris, God bless. Love Jack, James, Tracey, Mick and families xxxx.'

Meghana continued to type into the Family Announcements screen while Aaeesha kept flicking through *Heat*.

'And would you like any artwork?'

'Sorry duck?'

'Some people like to have a picture of something, like an urn, or angels or something, to go next to the obituary.'

'Oh right ...'

'It doesn't cost any extra.'

'Oh right, well then you might as well chuck in a couple of angels.'

'Okay, two angels.'

'Yes duck.'

Meghana clicked onto the artwork box and selected two angels, which on closer inspection weren't actually angels, because the very cheap art package that the *Evening Post* had bought did not contain any angels, only cupids from a previous valentine package with zeros attached to their heads. Part of her thought it wasn't right that the recently deceased should be immortalised by a symbol that was possibly classical, or possibly even capitalist, instead of a Christian one – even though she herself had never been a Christian – but another bored or rebellious part of her thought well, what the hell did it matter?

Family Announcements constitutes the largest section of the *Nottingham Evening Post*'s Classified Advertisements (even though it isn't, strictly speaking, advertisements), and consists, primarily, of obituaries, many of which are illustrated with an amalgamation of classical and capitalist imagery. My study explores the ways in which the incorporation of these economic symbols impacts upon the religious landscape of the East Midlands area through a case-by-case approach ...

'Now let me just read that back to you. "Bradley, Iris. Much-loved sister-in-law and favourite Auntie who always made us smile. A genuine woman who we will always love and remember. Goodnight Iris, God bless. Love Jack, James, Tracey, Mick and families xxxx." And then two angels. Is that right?'

'Yes duck.'

'It'll be in tomorrow night's paper. Thank you. Goodbye.'

Meghana pressed 'end call' then clicked back onto www.blueyonder.co.uk and typed 'meginthefield' into the username box, followed by 'methefieldstudy' into the password box beneath it. She saw that there was one new message from Dave, which she opened:

Dear Post-Meg,

I am emailing you from my brand new laptop (!!!). Check this out: https://www.youtube.com/watch?v=w_BkcCPOd5M

And let me know if you fancy a drink later.

Love, Dave Workshop

Which translated as:

Dear Post-Meg,

I am emailing you from my brand new laptop (!!!). Check this out: https://www.youtube.com/watch?v=w_BkcCPOd5M

And let me know if you fancy a drink later.

Love, Dave Workshop

Because nothing in my life ever changes, thought Meghana, resentfully. Yet, as there wasn't anything else lighting up the switchboard, she clicked on the link, and a video of a hooded, kneeling man appeared. At first glance it was so like all of the other awful images that had been filling up the Internet that she automatically placed it too in the category of violence, and accordingly her immediate response was to gasp out loud.

'What the fuck?' said Aaeesha, leaning over her shoulder.

'I-I-I don't understand.' And then she realised that the man wasn't actually being tortured; rather he was wearing a hood, or more specifically a monk's habit, and that it was this detail alone that resembled the news.

Meghana looked more closely and saw that the man was kneeling down in order to rearrange the letters on a scrabble board while five other men, on five different TV monitors, each chanted the words of a different pop song. What looked like incense sticks were burning in a jam jar, and a strange purple symbol had been painted on the floor. The caption underneath it read, 'A kaos magik ritual involving video-conferencing and the use of discordiant images, sounds and smells.'

'Don't worry, it's just Dave being an idiot,' said Meghana.

'Then why do you hang out with him?'

'Because I'm a different but compatible type of idiot.'

'Right . . .'

'What I mean is—'

'Do you know what I'd love to try?' came Judy's voice from behind them, and in response Meghana immediately clicked back onto the Family Announcements screen.

'No,' she said, attempting to look busy. 'Please tell me.'

'Some Indian sweets. I've heard that they're absolutely delicious.'

'Well, yeah, I mean you get different types in different areas.'

'Made with sweetened milk and pistachios and—'

'I think that's mainly in the north.'

'And something called—'

'Hello, Family Announcements. Aaeesha speaking how can I help you?' said Aaeesha, much more loudly than normal.

'And something called gram flour and—'

'Okay, I'm just going to read that back to you using the phonetic alphabet to check that I've got the correct spelling. That's Sarah – Sierra, Alpha, Romeo, Alpha, Hotel . . .'

'And cardamom – that's very popular isn't it? And—'

'I'll bring some in for you,' Meghana almost shouted, while simultaneously trying to push all thoughts of a discordiant, or even discordant, smell to the furthest corner of her mind.

'Oh would you?' And Judy shook the tin of shortbreads, first at her, and then Aaeesha. 'Now wouldn't that be nice!'

Deuteronomy

KATARZYNA KWIATKOWSKA STOOD ON A chair in the centre of her parents' living room, while her mother and Mrs Jones from next door crouched at her feet. Then she raised her arms above her head and touched the lampshade that dangled from the ceiling and, as she did so, she wondered why the man that they were making her wedding dress for no longer replied to her emails; and then she wondered why, in spite of this fact, she was still glad that they were making her wedding dress now, or maybe she was just glad that they were here with her now, in this little patterned room that, unlike her flat in Forest Fields, which was only white and now also cold, was always warm and cosy ...

'Stop moving arms about,' said Iwona. 'Or you will get the prick with pin.'

'Your mum's right love,' said Mrs Jones. 'We need to make sure it's hanging properly.'

Katarzyna put her hands on her hips and then held her breath until she turned into a white marble statue in underwear that wasn't quite white because it had been washed with her black tights and jumpers because when it came to her underwear she just didn't care. Just as she didn't care if she got lines on her face from worrying, or fat from sitting down all day, because although when she touched the lampshade and looked up she felt as if she were about to break out into something bigger and larger and

93

more fulfilling than just herself, as soon as she dropped her arms she knew that in reality she was falling . . .

'This is good now, yes?' said Iwona, and Mrs Jones, after tugging at the hem, also nodded. 'Kasia, say the thank you to Mrs Jones.'

'Thank you Mrs Jones.'

'I think you're old enough to call me Carol now love,' said the woman who was now called Carol. 'So when's the wedding taking place then?'

'That is very good question,' said Iwona.

Katarzyna wriggled her fingers but retained her grey-and-white pose. She and Eoin had talked about dates before he went away, and then she had talked to Canon Zawodniak up at the Cathedral, and even, under her mother's duress, to the priest at the Polish Mission – because even though they all, supposedly, belonged to one holy, Catholic and apostolic church, the priest up at the Polish Mission was much more old-fashioned and strict – and then she had emailed Eoin their suggestions. And then emailed him again . . .

'Well I emailed Eoin some dates.'

'These days wedding take long time because expectation are so high,' Iwona said darkly. 'These days girls want whole shebang.'

'And where will you get married?' said Carol.

'I don't care. I'd be happy with a registry office.'

Iwona patted the section of Katarzyna's leg that was closest to her, and inadvertently drove a pin into her thigh. Katarzyna winced but once again kept still. She watched as Iwona turned to Carol and in English said, 'She will marry in Polish Church or maybe even Cathedral.' And then looked up at Katarzyna and in Polish added, 'I didn't go to all this trouble for you to behave like a heathen in front of the neighbours.'

To which Katarzyna wriggled her fingers, and then in Polish said, 'I'm not a heathen, I'm a pagan.'

Which translated as:

I'm a Romantic.

Which translated as:

I believe in the divine character of the natural world and all the strange and wondrous power that this contains.

Which translated as:

And I still believe in love – natural, animal and pure – all of which exists outside of any institution ...

Then she looked at Carol and in English said, 'I think that the Cathedral would be a bit big, so probably the Polish Church – although Eoin's family go to St Flannan's.'

'Oh that's where my sister used to go. But now she lives in West Bridgford.'

'Kasia did GCSEs at English Martyrs,' said Iwona.

'But you didn't want to stay on?'

'She wanted the vocational training,' said Iwona, looking up at her daughter.

'I want to be a journalist,' said Katarzyna, looking down at her mother.

'Ah ...' said Carol, because, even if Katarzyna were to have explained her extensive, secret reading, it would still not quite have accounted for the many blank years prior to her enrolment at New College. 'Is that so ...?'

Iwona and Carol stood and began to circle Katarzyna, who remained as still as a white-and-grey statue, and took out some of the pins. Katarzyna looked up at the ceiling, and as she did so she remembered how she had only said 'yes' to Eoin because she had always said 'yes' to Eoin, just as she had always said 'no' to anything, besides her extensive, secret reading, that might have taken her away from anyone who dressed and spoke the same way he and she did; and then she looked down at the floor and wondered, once again, about that other bigger blacker 'no' that she equated with Eoin's silence now ...

Katarzyna clambered back down off her chair and twisted into her ugly tracksuit bottoms. Then she pulled her ugly tracksuit top back over her head, and then, only when she was sure that she wasn't going to cry at the fact that her tracksuit was so ugly that it made her ugly too, emerged from out the other end.

'Thanks Mrs – I mean Carol. You've been very kind,' said Katarzyna, as Iwona helped her to find her coat.

'It's no bother at all love. Just don't forget my invitation!'

The three of them laughed politely, and then Carol let herself out. A second later, the echo of her own front door opening and closing vibrated through the wall. Iwona put the bag of fabric back inside her sewing box and Katarzyna fell down beside her on the settee. She was so tired that in spite of her earlier efforts she started crying, and then she just carried on crying, until her eyes and her cheeks matched her mouth and her ugly tracksuit and she was just one giant sobbing blob . . . And then she felt her mother's arms around her and heard her softer, Polish voice:

'When I first sought asylum I was terrified. I thought that I had made a huge mistake. I used to wake up in the night terrified that I would never learn English, or make friends, or find work. Sometimes I thought that I would be sent back and put in jail. But, most of all I was frightened because I thought that I would never see your dad again, and that I would have to have my baby on my own. But do you know what I did? I said my prayers. And I kept on trying. And, well, look at the three of us now – everything worked out just as it should.'

10.11.2004

I always carry a picture of my mother. She's wearing a blue dress and holding me in her arms. The writing on the back says that I'm four years old, which makes her the same age that I am now. I don't re-member it being taken, or much about her either for that matter, but otherwise there's only men to look at – fighting, or begging, or both.

Lingāchāra

KATARZYNA KWIATKOWSKA MADE HER WAY to the very back of the Evening Post Classifieds office, and positioned her rucksack so that no one other than Meg could sit beside her. She had spent the last few days wondering what her next film should be, and having recently seen a picture of the strange, phallic stone sculptures that, if she had understood the explanatory paragraph correctly, the Hindus worshiped three times each day, thought that this could be the starting point; and consequently, she wanted to ask Meg about this possible beginning to a possible extension of the 'Architecture of Belief' before her shift had ended.

Katarzyna put on her headset and looked at the little green light but decided not to press 'answer'. She had worked out that on average she received around ten calls an hour, which meant that on average she spoke to around seventy idiots a day – and today she just couldn't be bothered. Judy had already been waylaid by one of their usual problem callers, which left only Sam from Motors, who had a hangover, and Aaeesha Begum, who alternated between Family Announcements and handing out fudge. Accordingly, she pressed 'busy', and then began to type, very quickly, into the box on the Free Ads screen:

Three volumes of the Encyclopedia Britannica (Ba-Br, M and G) will swop for microwave if in good condition. Contact Paul, Long Eaton 9133446.

Then she typed 'www.hotmail.com' into the navigation bar, 'katarzyznastan' into the username box and 'eoineoineoin' into the password box beneath it. Then she pressed 'refresh', 'refresh', 'refresh' – but nothing. Then she clicked back to the Free Ads screen and carried on typing:

Selection of computer games including Grand Theft Auto and Battlefield Vietnam will swop for train tickets (Southern locations preferred). Contact Steve, Nottingham 9476342.

A variety of things in jars will swop for BMW. No time wasters please. Contact Ann, Mansfield 9186541.

A variety of things in jars will swop for a selection of items in boxes. Contact Mike, Nottingham 9148283.

Then she clicked back to www.hotmail.com. Then she pressed 'refresh', 'refresh', 'refresh' again – but nothing. Katarzyna sighed. She had already forgotten the Hindu sculptures and gone back to not forgetting Eoin, for whom she was just about to begin an Internet search, when Judy came over. She looked down at the Free Ads screen, which glimmered conscientiously in front of them, nodded approvingly at it and said, 'Have you had some of Aaeesha's fudge yet?'

Katarzyna also nodded at the screen. 'No, not yet I'm afraid. I've been too busy.'

'Well you must try some when you get the chance, it's absolutely delicious, although,' Judy lowered her voice confidentially, 'it is rather a shame that she didn't bring any of her own food in.'

'But didn't she just go on holiday to Devon? I mean isn't Devon like famous for fudge?'

But before Judy had the chance to reply, the little green light started flashing.

'Hello, Evening Post Swop Shop. Kathy speaking how can I help you?'

She started typing into the Free Ads screen, while staring straight ahead, until Judy went on her way again. Then, as soon as the call had ended, she clicked onto Google and searched for Eoin's name, followed by 'When will the war in Iraq be over?' and 'Why is the war in Iraq taking so long?' before realising that she needed to be both more and less specific. She adjusted her baseball cap and then googled 'British troops in Basra latest', and to her surprise a YouTube link appeared.

Katarzyna clicked on the YouTube link and an Arab man started writhing on the floor. A circle of white men dressed in khaki surrounded him, all of whom were taking it in turns to hit him on his face, back and stomach. They were all laughing, while one of them threatened to rape his sister while he watched. Then another said that they would rape him. Then another said that if he didn't talk they would arrest his mother and do the same to her. Then he said that they would do it anyway. One of the men had Eoin's laugh.

Katarzyna sat, motionless, while the tiny, violent rectangle continued to pulse and flicker in the place that should have been the Free Ads screen. She could see Aaeesha making her way towards her and yet she felt powerless to stop whatever it was that was playing out in front of her now. She watched as Aaeesha reached her desk, held out the box of fudge, and then heard her say: 'Want one?'

Katarzyna stared through Aseesha and into the computer, and her mind went as white and cold as her flat without Eoin, and then her throat went dry. She knew that she should click onto a different screen but she had forgotten how to use her fingers.

'I-I-I—'

'They're made with clotted cream, not so good for your waistline, but still.'

'I, err ...'

'I brought them back from ...'

Aaeesha followed Katarzyna's gaze back into the computer. Then they both watched, in silence, as the Arab man raised the dark, bruised pulp that had once been his face up towards the khaki circle. His broken mouth was covered in wet and dry blood, which was red and black and brown. He started to cry, and then to scream: 'Allahu Akbar! Allahu Akbar!' while all the men continued laughing.

'I-I-I'm sorry,' said Katarzyna.

Aaeesha turned and looked at her, and Katarzyna looked back, for the first time properly. She saw that the hijab framing Aaeesha's face made her appear curiously ageless. And then she saw Aaeesha looking back at the screen and then back at Katarzyna and then dropping the box of fudge, so that all of the soft little blocks of fat and sugar rolled out across the floor. And then she saw her put her hands up over her mouth and slowly repeat: 'Allahu Akbar.'

Sadāchāra

MEGHANA BUDANNAVAR ENTERED THE GROUNDS of Nottingham University and walked up past the lake that, during the summer term, was filled with rowing boats; past the kiosk that, during
the summer term, sold ice creams; and past the rhododendron
bushes that, during the summer term, were covered in large, almost tropical pink flowers. She knew that her parents had actually met here, as medical students, and not in their hometown of
Bangalore; and consequently she wondered whether these, to her
mind, inferior rhododendron bushes had therefore seemed more
or less exciting to them than those that, back in India, blazed all
the way from Kanyakumari to the Himalayas ...

She twisted a long strand of hair around her index finger and
carried on walking until she reached the entrance to the geography department and the warm bureaucratic corridors filled
with people who didn't even know how to use the Internet and
still relied on filing. Then she went inside and made her way towards the room at the far end, knocked, and waited for the familiar squeak of floorboards. There was silence, followed by a short,
woody croak, and a second later, Professor Woźniak opened the
door, and said, 'Ah Meg, good to see you. Come in, come in, sit
down.'

He gestured to the empty seat in front of him while his eyes
moved briefly over her. Instinctively, Meghana drew her coat

around her shoulders, and then, with one hand raised towards her collar, took a seat; all the while the inward, ironical voice kept speaking, lifting her out of, and distancing her from, the warm, stuffy world that surrounded her:

Meghana Budannavar occupies an attractive, although, imaginary space, almost existing between the East Midlands and Bangalore. Her national identity is British (although her ethnicity is Indian); her gender is female (and likewise she regards her sexuality as a passive yet fluid occurrence); her age range is 16–24 (just); and her religion or belief is mainly Hindu (or, more specifically, Lingayat) but sometimes No Religion and sometimes Other (although she is unwilling, or perhaps unable to specify exactly what she might mean by this, her last vague statement). Our study explores Meghana's impact as a supposedly exotic (but neither daring, romantic nor poetic) fixture in the anthropology bit of the geography department where partial funding is available ...

'So Meg ...' said Professor Woźniak.
'Yes?'
'So, uh, yes ...'
'My notes?'
'Uh yes, your notes.'
Professor Woźniak began to look up at her, with what appeared to be the intention of looking up and down at her, but then stopped and gave one of his piles of papers, which she now realised were actually her notes, a final sublimated shuffle.
'So it uh ...' Having exhausted his shuffling he now stroked his moustache. 'It seems like your focus has changed ...?'
'Yes?'
'To an, uh, to a more symbolic and interpretive one?'
'Well I suppose that I've been thinking more about belief.'
'Yes?'
'Belief as part of a system, which in turn creates meaning.'
'Yes?'
'So I was thinking that if we move away from a phenomenological approach, whereby we see the City of Caves not as a physical

network, but as a metaphysical one, formed by the actions of those who visit it now as much as those who lived there in the past, and whose shared histories ...'

Professor Woźniak took out a cigarette and lit it, an action that reminded Meghana of how, when she had first encountered him, he had seemed rather a glamorous figure, and how, on account of his nationality, age and moustache, she had attributed to him the type of exotic past that she herself would have fled from. And then she smiled warmly and broadly at him and tried not to play with her hair ...

'Well firstly, I think that we need to remember that a phenomenological approach and a symbolic, or interpretive approach aren't mutually exclusive.' Professor Woźniak took a drag of his cigarette and flicked the ash with his yellow fingers. 'And as you well know, these days the lines between them are increasingly blurred. Secondly I'm not sure that what you're saying makes any kind of sense.'

Meghana nodded because she wasn't sure either, then looked through the window at the empty lake and the empty ice cream kiosk and the bare and inferior rhododendron bushes. She knew that everything that she had just said had nothing to do with her thesis but quite a lot to do with Dave, and then she remembered that he wanted to go with her to Leicester for Diwali, which would mean that something definite and so no longer safe was happening between them ...

'Do you remember David?' said Professor Woźniak.

Meghana twisted a strand of hair around her index finger and tugged hard at it. 'What?'

'I said do you remember David, David Goldstein? He used to be the Cross-Cultural Identities Research Group convener.'

'Yes I remember him.'

'Might be worth getting in touch. He did some interesting work on belief when he was here, although he now seems to have disappeared completely ...'

'He's managing the Games Workshop.'

'The what?'

'It's nothing.'

Meghana watched as Professor Woźniak wrote something down and handed it to her, and then she put it in her bag, stood up and said goodbye. She felt sad to already be leaving his smoke and warmth behind her, as well as the smoke and warmth of his office, which joined the anthropological bits and the historical bits and the theological bits of what constituted the geography department's giant filing system together. The university always seemed like such a different, cloistered world – both very big and very small but always very far away from what was real and solid – and very unlike her life outside of it, where everything became cold and clear again, and nearer to Dr David Goldstein, who used to be the Cross-Cultural Identities Research Group convener but now seemed to have disappeared completely . . .

Meghana left the building and walked into a large, forty-something man who, despite the weather, was clad only in a tee-shirt, the slogan on which boldly stated 'I'M ON THE LIST'. She looked at him and shivered, and the man looked back at her, and said, 'This isn't cold.' And then laughed to reveal a mouth filled with gold that, unlike her hair, or indeed any other part of her, inside or out, twinkled merrily.

Sivāchāra

STANISŁAW KWIATKOWSKI WALKED UP PAST the still, silver lake, the pale-pink ice cream kiosk, the glossy-green leaves of the rhododendron bushes, and towards Józek's office, where the squeaky floorboard, which plagued his tender ears, and which the university's maintenance department considered too small and insignificant a task to warrant their attention, was in need of Stanisław's friendly expertise. As he rounded the corner he saw a beautiful young woman, shivering in exactly the same, melancholy way that his daughter would have done had she been there now, and as a result of this he laughed and said, 'This isn't cold.'

The woman held his gaze for a moment, her long black hair streaked across the silver, pink and green, before walking silently away. He watched as she receded, then shook his head and checked his watch. He was early, so he wandered off towards Starbucks. He liked the big leatherette armchairs and the wood-effect panelling, both of which reminded him of someone else's home; and he also liked the girl who worked behind the counter, who, unlike the woman he'd passed just now, or even his wife, or even his daughter, always smiled when she saw him.

'Hello Stan. Nice tee-shirt,' said the girl as soon as he entered.

'Thank you. I am what you call the joker, yes?'

'Well it's certainly brightened up my day.'

'Again, thank you. And now I would like the white coffee.'

'Do you mean Americano?'

'Americano is coffee, yes?'

'Yes.'

'It is white, yes?'

'If you add a dash of milk yes.'

'No other ingredients?'

'No.'

'Then yes I mean Americano. And by the way you have nice smile.'

The girl smiled nicely and typed something into the till.

'And would that be a grande Americano?'

'No, small.'

'Small is tall.'

'No small is small.'

'No small is tall,' she said again, still smiling, and then began to fiddle with the coffee machine's nozzle, until it squirted coffee and steam into an officially small or tall but actually massive paper cup. 'Okay so that's one tall Americano! Here you go! Enjoy!'

Stanisław took his coffee from her, added a dash of milk and sat down. Opposite him two boys were drinking out of officially grande but actually colossal paper cups, each one of which was filled with syrup and cream, so that as they raised their drinks towards their mouths their lips became covered in foam, turning them both into babies.

'Well there's a march next week, and I really think that we should go,' said one of them.

'But what's the point?' said the other. 'The march last year was the biggest march, the biggest protest, in human history—'

'According to who?'

'According to everyone. And the news. And it didn't do anything. We can't do anything. We're powerless.'

The first boy became aware of the foam, and wiped his mouth with the back of his sleeve. Then he pulled out a bag of badges, like the ones that Dave, and now also Katarzyna wore, and placed them on the centre of the table.

'But even if we can't stop it we can still show that we don't agree with it. And that's doing something, surely?'

'Yes, if doing something means making yourself feel better. But if doing something means helping others, then no.'

The second boy took another sip of cream and syrup, while his friend looked at the badges that had now spilled out between them.

'My father was killed in 1970,' said Stanisław suddenly.

Both of the boys turned round. There was a long pause and then eventually the first one said, 'Killed?'

'Yes. During riot. At that time condition in shipyard very bad. The workers riot. My father killed. But it change nothing. Later we form Solidarność. It mean solidarity – a union of workers but separate to state – and then in '81 Solidarność strike. I strike. And this time government bring in army.'

The first boy nodded dumbly, while the second boy dipped his index finger into what remained of his drink and sucked on it like a dummy.

'After eight years more, communism end. For some people there is now freedom, yes? It is easier to leave Poland, to work in other country, yes? But this is because of what happen in 1970 and 1981, even if seem like nothing happen at some times.'

The second boy took his finger out of his mouth and said, 'Well that's certainly given us something to think about. Thanks for sharing.'

Stanisław looked back at the girl behind the counter and sighed, and then took a sip of coffee that was suddenly bitter. He knew that these boys, who had now turned away from him, didn't understand him, and that they couldn't understand him. He knew that to them and people like them he would never be anything more than an eccentric, amusing foreigner, or worse still an annoying one – and yet the old words, Wałęsa's words, which now came back to him, were not ones he could forget: 'I do not want to but I have to.'

Reluctantly, the second boy turned back.

'Please,' said Stanisław, 'I would like the badge.'

The boy picked one up and handed it to Stanisław, who pinned it onto his tee-shirt so that it made a dot above the 'i' in 'list', and as he did so the urge to share what he knew, to try, once more, and make them understand continued to rise up, unexpectedly, inside him, so that, before the boy had time to turn away again, Stanisław had taken hold of his shoulder. He held on, very tightly and then, pushing his face close said, 'The Pope support Wałęsa, support Solidarność,' and on this, last word he clenched his hand into a fist and held it in the air, 'and the Pope also want to stop this war. This is good, yes? This is what hope mean, yes?'

Bhrityāchāra

DR DAVID GOLDSTEIN EDGED INTO the only available parking space and looked up at the large red-brick building that might once have been a house, or a pub, but now, thanks to the various stone sculptures that had been attached to the top half of it, functioned as a Hindu temple. Then he turned, perhaps a little too eagerly, to Meg, who was sitting, shivering, in the passenger seat beside him, and said, 'This err, this must be it.'

'Must be.'

'Err . . .'

'Well come on then.'

He couldn't help feeling a little disappointed, not only by Meg's current lack of enthusiasm, but also the numerous ways in which she had consistently skirted his attempts to visit Leicester for Diwali – which meant that she still didn't want him to meet her family, which meant that she still didn't want him to be part of her family, which meant that anything more than a drink after work was still resolutely out of bounds. He watched as she opened the door of his parents' car, and stepped out onto the street, and shivered again, from what he assumed must be the darkness more than the cold.

'But are you sure we've got the right day?' he said, clambering out after her.

'No. No I'm not. I've never been to this temple, and I don't keep track of such things.'

'But what are the rules?'

'Be a good Hindu.'

'But there must be others.'

'Yes, if you like.'

Meg buttoned up her coat, and then they walked, in silence, up towards the entrance, where an old lady in a sari and an anorak was handing out sweets.

'I should take some for Judy,' said Meg.

'Who's Judy?'

'This really annoying woman at work.'

'Oh?'

But nothing more was forthcoming. David took one of the sweets and then wondered what he should do with it. He thought that it seemed rude to refuse the old lady, but also wrong to start eating, and yet, as soon as he put the soft white ball inside his pocket, where it immediately squashed against his thigh, he regretted his earlier worries. He noticed that Meg, who hadn't taken a sweet, was removing her shoes, and so quickly followed suit, before, as always, trailing after her . . .

'But there's no order,' said David, as the temple, meaning the statues, the carvings, the general excesses, rose up, abruptly, all around him.

'What do you mean?'

'I don't know.'

'Well that's not much of an answer.'

He reddened and looked at the floor, thinking as he did so that although he wanted to articulate how unsettled he was feeling, the only thing he could have put into words was that the sensation of walking on the polished marble in just his socks struck him as unusual. He could see shrines, or what he assumed were shrines, dotted at what looked like random intervals – not just on the sides of the walls but throughout the whole of the space. And he could see that each one of them contained several black stone statues, wearing real, but miniature clothes and decorated with fresh flowers. And he could see that incense and oil lamps were burning in the alcoves in front of them, and that in between them were plates laid out with the soft white sweets, fresh fruit and yet more flowers . . .

David stepped closer to the nearest shrine, and as he did so he realised that his socks were soggy. He looked down and saw that a large tap was attached to the base, and that, although nothing was coming out of it now, it clearly had done recently. Then a bare-chested man, adorned with ash, vilva leaves and sandal paste drifted past, and the creamy, precious scent engulfed him . . .

'And what are they?'

He pointed to the bits of fruit, eager for names, terms, through which to understand it all, and yet deep down he also knew that whatever words he found would still not come close to what he wished to think of as the experience's centre.

'Pieces of fruit?' said Meg, twisting her hair around her long, elegant fingers. 'Incense? Lamps? Some of the same sweets that you put in your pocket earlier?'

The bare-chested man drifted by again, and this time offered up a fragrant smile, while David shook his dripping foot, and then looked at Meg imploringly. He wanted, more than anything else, to say, 'I love you and I want to be your lover,' but instead he blurted out, 'Sometimes I don't want to be your friend.'

'I was only being stupid. You don't need to take offence,' said Meg, and then, pointing to the fruit and to the sweets, 'Deepa and naivaedyaas, for the statues that represent the different gods that represent the different aspects of the one god Brahman.'

'Well that's a very thorough answer.'

'So does that mean that you still want to be my friend?'

'Yes, yes . . . I-I just, err—' But still he couldn't say it.

Instead he looked back towards the shrine nearest to him, now noticing how the flowers that decorated some of the smaller statues had been upturned and placed upon their heads. The bare-chested man drifted by again, and then some children came in and stood in front of another shrine – but still it made no sense.

'And what are they?' he said, pointing at the upturned flowers.

'Sun hats?' Meg laughed, and then quickly added, 'I mean I

don't know, just another way of decorating the statues I suppose, but I don't think they have a special name or anything.'

'Oh.'

'Are you disappointed?'

'No,' he said, which was partly true because of all the beauty that surrounded him, but partly false because he had failed to act when the moment inside him had arisen.

David looked around the temple, and just like his visits to the cathedral or the synagogue, what he saw made no sense. He could not conceive of any rules or order, and yet the place smelled of sandalwood and fruit and leaves, and some of the statues, the ones that represented the different gods that represented the different aspects of the one god Brahman, wore flowers like tiny sun hats on their black stone heads. And some of the women, specifically Meg, had long, silky hair and long, silky eyelashes. It was beautiful, yes, it was beautiful, so beautiful that for a moment he became lost in it – but still it made no sense . . .

'Even Kathy has started asking me about my heritage,' said Meg, stressing the last word to make it sound ridiculous. 'She wants to make a film about the lingam.'

'That's interesting. I mean I don't understand all . . .' His gaze drifted back towards the bare-chested man, 'all, err, all this. But it's beautiful.'

Meg laughed again, and then suddenly stopped and pulled her coat around her even tighter than before, even though the temple, like the darkness, wasn't cold.

'Everything's just a look to you though isn't it Dave? And the browner and weirder the better?'

And then they were back to the mood of their arrival. He felt disappointed, both with Meg's reluctance to be near him, and his failure to bridge the gap that existed between them. He thought not only of the sweet sticking to the inside of his jeans and his soggy socks but also that there had to be some way out of it, to love, or at least impress her.

'Actually, I've been doing some more research into magik – you know, with a "k", and I was hoping to organise something pretty special, a kind of religious experiment almost. It would take three of us to do it, three magicians, and together we'd kind of harness the Internet, use it as a kind of transmitter to transmit, I don't know, err, love maybe, which could be in a platonic or even an, err, romantic sense. And I was wondering if you could have a word with Kathy about using the Media Hub and—'

'No.'

Meg scraped her hair back into an elastic band and did up the last button on her coat.

'Well okay then, I suppose I could email her—'

'No Dave, no. I mean ... I mean, it's like I sometimes think that you'd rather be Kathy's friend than my friend. But Kathy's Eoin's friend.'

'But isn't she engaged to Eoin?'

Meg was still beautiful when she was angry, thought David, but he preferred her when she wasn't. Plus, she made no sense. And yet now she too smelled of sandalwood and fruit and leaves – things he didn't yet know the reasons for, or even where or how to learn them. He was just an educated Englishman, he told himself sadly, all too aware of his type of existence, its multiple meanings and multiple truths all of which had been discussed, at length, during the Cross-Cultural Identities Research Group, but none of which ever culminated in anything more than a footnote or two on appropriate contexts ...

He took a deep breath, and as he did so he reminded himself that you could be the Cross-Cultural Identities Research Group convener or the Games Workshop Manager one day, but an almighty wizard the next. Or a PhD nerd one day and an almighty wizard the next. Or even the lover of the one you loved, and who just might, with a little persuasion, be persuaded to love you too, and as if by some kind of magik ...

And then in one small-but-big-enough-to-be-reckless moment David reached out for Meg, held onto her, and kissed her.

Ganāchāra

MARGARET O'SHEA STOPPED, STOOPED AND rubbed her knees, which as always ached. Then, when she stood up again, the sudden rush of blood to the head made her dizzy. She held out one arm, palm flat against the wall, and waited until the feeling had passed, and then, when she was just about right again, she put the teapot on the tray, rearranged the plate of bourbon creams and shuffled back into the front room, where Blessings and Albertina were waiting.

'Let me help you with that,' said Blessings.

She took the tray from her, while Albertina plumped up one of the already plump cushions.

'Thank you.' Margaret made a breathy whistling sound. 'But you're the visitor Albertina, so it really should be me who is helping you.'

Albertina smiled at Margaret and then at Blessings, who, like her, had recently joined the St Vincent de Paul Society, which meant that they were now responsible for visiting the sick and elderly members of the parish. As Margaret did not see herself as either of these things, however, she had decided that the only option was to view their visit as amusing, or even, if you took the 'de' into account, just a little bit affected.

'And how are your knees Margaret?' said Blessings.

'Oh they're fine, fine thank you, yes.'

Margaret looked down at her legs and realised that, without thinking, she had just given them another rub. Then she removed her hearing aid and put it in her pocket, picked up the plate of bourbon creams, and held it out in front of her.

'Now ladies please, you must help yourself to a *bourbon*.' And both Blessings and Albertina took one, while Margaret smiled knowingly.

'Albertina is going to Lourdes soon. Perhaps she could bring you back some holy water?' said Blessings, taking a second biscuit already.

'Yes of course, Margaret. For your knees,' said Albertina.

'My knees are fine thank you Albertina,' said Margaret, almost irritably, and then immediately added, 'I mean to say, is this the first time that you've been to France?'

'Well I—'

'Margaret would like to go to Paris,' said Blessings, while Margaret tried her hardest not to glare at her.

'You just all seem to be so fond of all things French that's all.'

'Well French is my first language,' said Albertina. 'French and Kinyarwanda. I only knew a little English when I first arrived, although since I did I have been studying hard.'

'At New College,' Blessings cut in. 'Albertina has just completed Access to English.'

'Level Five,' Albertina said proudly.

'Level Five,' Margaret repeated, with something a little like awe.

She looked at the blue statuette, in the hope of being comforted, and then fumbled in her pocket for her rosary. She had only managed three sets of mysteries before her visitors had arrived, which meant that she still had luminous to go.

'Perhaps you ladies would like to say the rosary with me?'

Blessings and Albertina nodded, and each produced their own set of beads from their handbags. And then the three of them bowed their heads and began to work their way through their first Our Father. They mumbled both apart and together for quite some time, and then they finished the rest of their tea.

'Now are you ladies sure you've had enough to eat?' said Margaret, and once more held out the plate towards them.

'I am very full now thank you Margaret,' said Albertina.

'Blessings?'

'I am full too.' And then, seeing Margaret getting rather unsteadily to her feet, she again took hold of her. 'Here let me help you.'

'No, no you're the visitors.'

'But we have come from St Vincent de Paul.'

'But you're not actually French!'

Albertina gave her a puzzled look while Blessings took the tray and, in spite of Margaret's protestations made her way towards the kitchen, before returning a few minutes later drying her hands on her skirt. Then she reached for her coat and Albertina, taking this as her cue to get going, stood up also and began to gather her things.

'Goodbye Albertina. Goodbye Blessings. Thank you for coming,' said Margaret, moving shakily towards the door.

'Goodbye Margaret. Thank you for the tea,' said Blessings.

'I will remember the holy water,' said Albertina.

Margaret smiled and then shut the door behind them, using all the locks and bolts. Then she sat back down, and felt both sad and happy to be on her own again. She stayed where she was for a moment, with one hand still touching the rosary tangled around the hearing aid in her pocket, and then she shuffled all the way upstairs to what was still Eoin's room.

She sat down, switched on the computer and typed 'www. google.com' into the navigation bar, which, as Kathy had explained to her, was a 'search engine', and then 'British troops in Basra latest', because that was the only thing that Margaret could think of, or wanted to search for, and then a YouTube link appeared. She clicked on the YouTube link and a succession of images, too unexpected to be true, flashed before her eyes like something from the Book of Revelation. She saw wet blood and dry blood and red and brown and black blood and screaming and crying in a room that might be in the desert or the mountains or still be beside the sea, or anywhere else where there was a gap for the suffering, which should have been shut up tight, to wriggle in and hurt her . . .

Margaret stopped looking and stood up again, and the sudden rush of blood to the head made her dizzy. She held out one arm, palm flat against the wall, and waited until the feeling had passed, and then, when she was just about right again, she shuffled out onto the landing. She could hear a funny noise coming in through the letterbox, but it didn't really register, because all that she could think about was the noise from the YouTube link that had hummed and buzzed across the screen, and was now humming and buzzing inside her head like a peculiarly violent tinnitus . . .

Margaret touched her ear, which, with or without her hearing aid, resonated with the low, rumbling sound of her grandson's laughter, and then tried to concentrate on the other noises that were coming into her front room now – except that she still felt dizzy. So she held out one arm, palm flat against the wall, and waited for the feeling to pass. Except that it didn't pass. It filled her mind and her mouth and her heart with something far bigger than she was, and then she felt herself falling . . .

Charge Sheet for Trial
by General Court Martial:
The Queen vs Eoin O'Shea

A CHARGE SHEET IS A formal document of accusation submitted to a court martial, a judicial system that tries defendants for breaches of military discipline. Once it has been submitted, between three to seven officers and warrant officers (depending on the seriousness of the offence) will then determine the guilt of the accused, and if found guilty the Judge Advocate will decide upon their punishment. This particular Charge Sheet refers to defendant 114285315, Corporal Eoin O'Shea, the Mercian Regiment, attached to the 1st Battalion.

STATEMENT OF OFFENCE:
Committing a civil offence contrary to Section 70 of the Army Act 1955, that is to say a war crime contrary to Section 51 of the International Criminal Court Act 2001, namely inhuman treatment of a person protected under the provisions of the Fourth Geneva Convention 1949 as defined by article 8(2)(a)(ii) of Schedule 8 of the said International Criminal Court Act 2001 and the International Criminal Court Act 2001 (Elements of Crimes) Regulations 2001.

APPENDICES:
1. Insert date of the offence.
2. Insert time of the offence.
3. Insert, if appropriate, citation of relevant provisions.

Slaanesh

Charge Sheet for Trial
by General Court Martial:
The Queen vs Eoin O'Shea

MARGARET O'SHEA WANDERED THROUGH THE darkness and into a memory of her childhood that, were it ever to be translated into film, would most likely win an award at Cannes. The opening shot was of bright, emerald green fields, lit with a fading, early evening light. A curl of smoke rose from behind a tiny cottage in one distant corner of the frame, while a hare lolloped in the foreground of another. There was no noise, other than wind and sometimes birdsong, and then after a minute or so the sound of Margaret's footsteps, which were uneven because of her shoes, one of which was two sizes too big.

Margaret saw the fields and the cottage and the smoke and the hare and then looked down at her shoes. She remembered that she was fifteen years old, and that the little cottage was her home. She reached the cottage, which had a floor made from beaten earth, and not enough glass for all of the windows, and then went inside to find her mother. She remembered that she was the oldest child who hadn't died, which meant that she needed to keep an eye on all the other, younger children who also hadn't died, which meant that she needed to keep an eye on seven children, some of whom were sick. Margaret found her mother and took the newest baby from her, and then her mother went outside and poked at something that was cooking on the fire ...

Margaret wandered on a few more years and into a little country church with wild roses growing round the entrance to it as well as the statue of Our Lady. She could see her family, not just her immediate family, but her first and second cousins and their first and second cousins and so on, opening out and out until all the people were both barely and probably family but had all come along anyway, because that was what you did at weddings. She could see the man who was about to become her husband, Steven O'Shea, waiting for her at the altar. Who like her father was also a labourer. And who like her father had left school at twelve years of age. And who like her father, her mother and everyone else she knew had grown up the same place she had. And spoke with the same accent she did. And although she hardly knew him, she knew that she would love him because she could see that he was not afraid. She could see that he was not afraid and yet he understood the world the same way she did, and that was something precious, golden, holy, she was sure . . .

Suddenly Margaret felt a great pain, but she knew that she would be alright because Steven had gone to fetch the midwife. Steven and Margaret didn't have any money because nobody had any money but Margaret had always kept their cottage, which was very like her parents' cottage, very clean, because she was very clean as well as being very proud. Margaret remembered how she had made their sheets from sewing flour sacks together, but how afterwards she had had to bleach the sacks to make sure that the writing didn't show, so that the midwife, when she came, wouldn't know that they couldn't afford real sheets. Margaret wanted to cry but she didn't cry because she was proud, and instead she let the pain wash over her for what seemed like days. And then, just as suddenly, it ended. And her daughter, Katherine, was in her arms. And Steven was allowed to come back in again and hold his daughter too. And even though the sheets were bloody, she knew that it would be alright because she could bleach them . . .

Margaret moved into a terrace in Belfast because Steven had got a job working in one of the shipyards. She wasn't sure how that could have happened what with her and Steven being

Catholics, unless of course he hadn't told them. It was wrong, the way the English took the Irish land, and the Irish jobs and the Irish money. It was wrong the way the English took everything they had. But they had taken it, and they were determined to keep on taking. So Margaret held her beads, and shut her eyes, and said her prayers for her husband and her daughter. And she kept on and on every day, shutting her eyes, until there was a knock at the door. And then there was the priest. And his voice was trembling. And he said there had been an accident – only she knew it wasn't true, because these accidents, which kept on happening to Catholic men in decent jobs, only ever happened to Catholic men in decent jobs, until there weren't any Catholic men in decent jobs left to do a decent job for anyone any more . . .

And then Margaret shot forward, out of Belfast and into the outskirts of Nottingham, and the maternity ward at the hospital where her daughter and her grandson waited. It was very different to when she'd had her baby. There were proper sheets on all the beds and free meals at meal times, and they let the men in too now, except that Katherine's man had gone away as soon as she fell pregnant, which meant that Eoin didn't even have his name, although he had Steven's name which meant that he was something fine, or fortunate, which meant that he was loved . . .

And then she was in another ward but this time Katherine was with lots of other people, all of whom were sick. And she kept on trying to tell the nurses that they should put her back on the maternity ward, but none of them would listen . . .

And then she wandered back into the little country church, which had also become St Flannan's, only this time there was nothing but a wooden box waiting for her at the altar, and this time the priest was saying, 'We gather here today to celebrate the life of . . .' Only the sound of the ticking clock made it impossible to tell if the name was 'Steven' or 'Katherine' or 'Eoin'. Margaret knelt down, took out her rosary and began to say the same words over and over, thinking as she did so of Steven or Katherine or Eoin, each one of whom was a different kind of mystery . . .

Margaret stood up and walked down the aisle towards the coffin. She was about to start singing, except that there was a clock in the background, which kept on ticking – slightly faster than a heartbeat and far too fast for hymns. Eleven ten, eleven eleven, eleven twelve – she felt the seconds and then the minutes jerking past. Eleven thirteen, eleven fourteen – and then she reached the wooden box and looked inside, but all there was was a soft pink mouth the exact same shade as Kathy's tracksuit, and then it opened up and said, 'Margaret are you there? Margaret it's me, it's—'

And then there was another, wailing sound that might have been a siren.

Nurgle

STANISŁAW KWIATKOWSKI UNSCREWED THE THERMOS flask that he had recently filled up with very strong tea, and poured out a small plastic cupful. He placed the cup on top of the tray that was fixed to the hospital bed and then said, 'Here Margaret. Proper tea.'

Margaret looked at him and as she did so her right eye flickered. The nurse had already explained that this was a normal reaction, and that she may also have some trouble with her short-term memory, and then she had smiled and said that with the right care and attention it would eventually sort itself out – a statement that had concerned Stanisław more than the ones that proceeded it, because who was there, besides his family, who could possibly give that to her?

'Very good.' Stanisław picked up the cup and held it up towards Margaret's lips. 'Strong, with lemon.'

Iwona reached out and put her hand, very gently, on his arm.

'Perhaps Margaret is not ready for the teas yet Stańko.'

Somewhere in the background came the sound of a baby crying, followed by the sound of footsteps, and then the curtains being drawn, hurriedly, around one of the other beds. Margaret shifted slightly, and then pulled herself up so that the numerous pillows that lay behind her splurged out around the sides.

'Is that Katherine?'

Iwona rearranged one of the pillows and reached for Margaret's hand. It was small, and soft as lace or tissue.

'Kasia has important appointment but she will be here again tomorrow.'

Yes, thought Stanisław, taking a sip of what should have been Margaret's tea, she'll be here again tomorrow, crying and blaming herself for something far beyond her – and yet there were so many other, better ways for a girl who was still so young and beautiful to live.

'Do you think that we should talk to the nurse?' said Stanisław to Iwona, in Polish. 'She can't rely on Kasia for everything – she's enough on her plate already.'

'But where's *my* Katherine?' said Margaret.

'She will be here tomorrow,' said Iwona.

'But is she in the maternity ward? Or the-the-the other ward?'

Margaret looked frightened, confused, and seeing this Iwona held her hand very firmly until all of the flickering stopped.

'I speak to Father Jonathan, he will visit tomorrow, yes?'

'Oh yes!' said Margaret, 'And will Blessings come too?'

'Please drink the tea Margaret, you need to keep up strength,' said Stanisław.

'But what about Blessings?'

'Father Jonathan will bless you,' said Iwona.

'Oh?'

'Yes many blessings.'

'But what about Blessings, you see she—'

'Please Margaret drink the teas,' Stanisław interrupted. 'I do not think you have enough of sugar in your blood.'

With a shaking hand Margaret raised the cup towards her lips, while Stanisław nodded approvingly. He knew that a woman from St Flannan's was meant to be bringing her communion later, but he was worried about how long afterwards she would stay, as well as how frequently the other old ladies would visit. The kind that supported her kind, which was almost the same as the kind that supported his kind, were dying out – and yet what was there, besides coffee shops, to replace them?

'Would you like something to eat Margaret? There is Starbucks downstairs,' he said, more softly.

With a not inconsiderable effort Margaret put the cup back down upon the tray.

'Oh no thank you Stan I'm fine, really. And I don't want to be any bother.'

Stanisław watched as Margaret's eyes flickered towards the Bible and the rosary beads lying next to a piece of paper on the bedside cabinet, and then up towards the television, suspended from a metal bar above her bed. She tried to smile and said, 'And I already have so much.'

'It is different from old days, yes,' said Iwona. 'Do you know, they even have the pets in children's ward now? So sick children also have to take the care of something.'

'I wonder what happened to Eoin's dog,' said Margaret.

'I did not know Eoin had dog?' said Stanisław.

Margaret nodded, and then began to whistle.

'In Iraq. It had a coat, but I don't know if it had a television.'

Stanisław took the cup of tea and placed it on the bedside cabinet. Without thinking he picked up the piece of paper, unfolded it and read:

1 – Hoover
2 – Wash up
3 – Make tea
4 – Say the rosary
5 – Arrange the flowers
6 – Send an email

'Stańko!' Iwona slapped him sharply on the wrist. 'Stańko you must not sneak through Margaret's things!'

'I am sorry. I-I-I was not thinking ...'

He folded the paper back up clumsily while Margaret continued to whistle at him.

'Honestly Stan it's fine. It's just the list that the occupational therapist made for me. She gets you to tell her all the things that you used to do each day and then she makes up exercises that remind your body how to do them.'

'That remind your body?'

'Yes. Because you know it never really forgets.'

Stanisław looked back down at the list. What was her life, he mused, but cooking, cleaning, praying, and now, a contemporary addition, most likely forced upon her by his daughter, sending an email to Eoin? But then what was wrong with that? Margaret's life might as well be his life, or if one was going to be pedantic, and include the cleaning, Iwona's. And yet their lives were still good lives and Margaret, as he could see, still laughed, or tried to . . .

'Mrs O'Shea?'

A young woman had entered the cubicle and was now standing at the end of the bed.

'Are you Blessings?' said Margaret.

'Is Blessings also black?' said the young woman.

'Yes. Are you her?'

'No, I'm Lucy. I'm one of the nurses.'

Iwona patted Margaret's hand and gave Lucy one of her firmest looks, while Lucy looked at the flask and frowned.

'And what's this?'

'Tea. Polish tea, with esencja,' said Stanisław.

'Eseni . . .'

'Esencja!'

He threw out his arms in a grand, theatrical gesture and Lucy began to laugh. Then she wrote something on a clipboard at the end of Margaret's bed, still laughing, and then he laughed also, winked and said, 'And by the way you have nice smile.'

Tzeentch

KATARZYNA KWIATKOWSKA SHIVERED, ZIPPED UP her puffa jacket, and continued to wander through the Market Square in what appeared to be a duck down duvet. There were little stalls all around her, designed to look like little wooden cottages, each of which contained German-themed Christmas goods, some of which were a bit like Polish goods except that they were more expensive. She knew that it was partly because the city wanted to appear European, and partly because it was twinned with Karlsruhe (as well as Ghent, Ljubljana, Minsk and Harare – although none of these places appeared to have travelling markets, or indeed a culture that could be commodified quite so easily).

She examined a series of wooden toys that struck her as having been designed more for the parents than their children, and wondered if she should buy one. Christmas was only a few weeks away but she still hadn't begun her shopping, because she still didn't know who to shop for. Should she still buy Eoin a present? And if she wasn't still buying Eoin a present then would it be weird to still buy Margaret one? And did everyone at the *Evening Post* really want or need a card?

She looked up at the digitally antiquated banner strung between two stalls. It said 'Frohe Weihnachten', which meant 'Merry Christmas' in German. In Polish people said 'Wesołych Świąt', and in Ireland 'Merry Christmas' – because no one who lived in

Ireland really spoke Irish anymore. It occurred to her that she didn't know what they said in Ghent, Ljubljana, Minsk and Harare, or even Basra for that matter. Or even if she cared. Except that of course she cared, because Eoin was out there, or somewhere thereabouts, and for better or worse she loved him ...

Katarzyna pulled up the hood on her puffa jacket, and continued to wander down through the Market Square dressed as the abominable snowman. She walked past a group of teenagers carrying placards, most of which depicted an enlarged version of her badge ('Stop the War', with two red bullet holes), although others held homemade versions that used old cardboard boxes – 'Stop the War, End Racism', 'Bush and Blair: Number One Terrorists' and even 'Bring Our Boys Home' – a sentiment that only a few days ago would have offered her some comfort, but which now felt vaguely threatening ...

She carried on walking very slowly, as if she didn't want to get where she was going, which she didn't, because she didn't want to get anywhere any more. But still she carried on walking, slower and even slower up towards New College, and while she walked she said the following rhyme:

Step on a crack
Break your back
Step on a line
Break your spine

She made her steps even smaller, as well as more deliberate, in exactly the same way that she remembered doing when she had walked to school, twisting her foot to one side and then the other in a weird and crooked way. The sky began to rumble and as she looked up to see what it was – a low-flying plane – she inadvertently stepped on a line. A shooting pain jabbed through her, and she shrieked with the suddenness of it ...

Katarzyna carried on walking up to the New College entrance, and then looked over her shoulder to check that no one else was watching. Students weren't meant to be in on a Sunday but Jackson had lent her his pass, which she now swiped, and went into the empty reception. A vase of dirty water and dead flowers, most of which were roses, sat on the empty desk, and as she looked at them she thought of all the different Polish words that, one way or another, meant dead. There was 'martwy', for example, for dead, or inanimate; and then there was 'zmarły' for dead, or departed; and then there was 'ślepy' for dead, or blind or implicit – and then she thought that any one of them would suit her better than her own name, which simply meant 'of flowers' . . .

Katarzyna walked down the steps and into the Media Hub. She took off her puffa jacket and attempted to turn it into a giant, marshmallow cushion with which to soften one of the uncomfortable chairs. Then she looked at the equipment, which seemed even smaller and more dead and blind than it usually did, before turning on all of the computers. She got out one of the video cameras and linked it up to one of the monitors, thinking as she did so that Meg and Dave were her only friends now, but that even they would hate her if they knew, if they didn't know already, because then they would know too that she was responsible. Because if she had loved harder, and loved better, she could have stopped this terrible thing from happening. Except she hadn't. And now all she could do was sit in the Media Hub, numb from her inferior loving, and wait for the instructions, the orders, that the people she hoped might still be her friends had promised or threatened to send her after she had replied, without thinking, to an email from Dave with the subject header 'favour' . . .

Katarzyna checked her phone and saw that she was half an hour early. Then she sat down on her coat that was now a cushion and typed 'www.hotmail.com' into the navigation bar, followed by her username, password and so on, and fifty-seven unread emails flashed onto the screen. She could see that some of them were from journalists, with subject headers that referred to justice, and torture, and British troops in Basra, but that most of them were from people she had never heard of, with subject headers that called her awful things, each and every one of which she was sure that she deserved. She wondered how they'd found her email, and then concluded that it must be from Facebook, which was something called a 'social networking site', which Jackson, eager that she too should have access to media, had suggested she join; and then she wondered how many people had seen the video on the Internet; and how long before the Internet would turn into the real news and everybody, not just kids and geeks, would read it, because it was printed in the proper papers ... Feeling numb and inferior, cold and loveless, she scrolled down the sidebar, ticking the box beside each one, and then she pressed 'delete'.

Katarzyna watched as all of the fifty-seven unread emails disappeared, and then she clicked 'refresh', and then 'refresh', and then 'refresh' – but nothing. And then she clicked 'new', and an empty box appeared. She cracked her knuckles, and tapped the keys – all of which added up to the following:

Dear Eoin,
    I don't care what you've done, I love you.
    Kathy x

She stared at it for what seemed like a long, long time and then thought about the way in which the layout of her email looked a little bit like the layout of a poem. Then she pressed 'delete' again, keeping her finger on the button until one by one all of the letters disappeared. Then she stared at the blank screen. Then she clicked 'cancel'. Then a little box popped up asking her whether she wanted to 'save draft' or 'delete'. She clicked 'delete'. Then another little box popped up, reminding her that she was about to throw away what had once looked a little bit like a poem but was now an empty space. She clicked 'continue'. And then she wondered if the Internet was trying to tell her something, namely that she needed to send a message from Katarzyznastan to Basra because one of them was under siege ...

Khorne

MEGHANA BUDANNAVAR WALKED UP TO the entrance of the
Evening Post Classifieds office, and then looked over her shoulder to check that no one else was watching. The office was always
shut on a Sunday, but she had managed to get hold of Judy's pass,
which she now swiped. She waited until the door made the bleep-
ing noise that meant the swipe had been successful, and then
she went inside. She removed her coat, which, she had now decided, had looked much better on her in the shop, and went into
the kitchen where a box of soft, white Indian sweets was going
mouldy by the kettle.

Meghana put the sweets in the bin and made herself a cup of tea,
with sugar but no lemon, because lemon would have been seen as
the wrong sort of foreign, which meant that it would have seemed
middle class and therefore snooty and so was not provided by *The
Post*. Then, while she waited for the kettle to boil, she thought about
how, in spite of her books and her hair and her clothes that never
seemed to do much for her, someone who had once been authori-
tative and distant, as opposed to unthreatening and merely familiar, obviously still saw her as attractive, as well as what this meant:

Dr David Goldstein holds a somewhat ambiguous appeal to those of the
opposite sex, simultaneously possessing great knowledge and author-
ity, and working as the Games Workshop Manager. His ethnic origin

is White or Jewish; his nationality is British; his gender is male; his age range is 25–34; and his religion or belief is No Religion or Other (magician). My study explores Dr Goldstein's impact as a supposedly unassuming (but subtly domineering) presence in the romantic landscape of my own, somewhat limited, imagination. Through a field study approach I will develop new methods for interpreting the key symbols and rituals that constitute Dr Goldstein's life, each one of which will not so much avoid as challenge pre-existing frameworks . . .

Meghana took a sip of tea and thought about how much of a relief it was to think about someone in the third person other than herself. It made her feel less mad which, as she wasn't daring or poetic or romantic enough to be mad in a daring or poetic or romantic way, was probably no bad thing. She looked out of the kitchen window at the canal, which in some places had frozen so that an upturned shopping trolley was now part suspended in the ice, and then into the mirror above the kitchen sink. As she moved closer to it she saw that she had one grey hair. She separated it out from all the others, pulled hard at it, and said, 'Ouch!'

Meghana checked the time on her phone and saw that there were still twenty minutes to go, and then she went and turned on one of the computers. She thought about how she had spent the last five years studying the science of humans and their works, and how she was now studying Dave the same way that Dave had been studying her. She thought that, after she had helped him to complete his experiment, which she still couldn't quite believe that she had agreed to be involved in, she would write it up, but with him, not it, as the subject. Then she would send it to him, explaining how it was now his turn to be her field study – except that actually she wouldn't, because deep down she didn't want to do anything that weird.

Meghana typed 'GoTeamBudannavar.blogspot.com' into the navigation bar, and a picture of her cousin's new baby appeared, with her cousin hovering in a contented blur behind him. Meghana looked at the picture and thought about how, these days, her own body seemed so separate from her – an assortment of oddments that, no matter what she did to them, or how she covered them, still never felt quite as they should. She typed 'Congratulations to Kajri! He's gorgeous. Already looks like another engineer to me! With love, Meghu x' into the comments box. And then she opened up the wide blue yonder, typed in her email, her password and all of the other usual things, and began to compose the following:

Dear Dave,
    While I am happy to take part in your 'magikal' experiment, please be aware that I am in the process of writing up my thesis. I realise that you may not have a problem with your current living and working arrangements, but I want to use my time productively.
    Remember: this is a one off, so don't get any ideas!
    Meg

She stared at it for a long time and then pressed 'delete', keeping her finger on the button until one by one all of the letters disappeared. Then she stared at the empty screen. And she began again:

Dear Dave,
    While I am happy to take part in your 'magikal' experiment on this one occasion, I really think that you could (and should) be doing something more productive with your time.
    Come on – you can do better than this!
    Meg

She checked the time on her phone and saw that there were still ten minutes to go, then pressed 'delete' again. And she began again:

Dear Dave,
    My parents are having a puja at their house next month for my cousin's baby. It's in Leicester obviously, but we can get cheap tickets if we book in advance.
    Hoping to cross cultural identities sometime soon,
    Meg X

All of which translated as something that was neither daring, nor poetic, nor romantic, but which might just about still do.

Meghana stared at the last email for a long time and then pressed 'delete', keeping her finger on the button until one by one all of the letters disappeared. Then she stared at the empty screen. Then she clicked 'cancel'. Then a little box popped up asking her whether she wanted to 'save draft' or 'delete'. She clicked 'delete'. Then another little box popped up, reminding her that she was about to throw away the empty screen without sending it. She clicked 'continue', and then she checked her phone and saw that, finally, it was time. She stood up, and with her shoulders hunched and her head lowered, took a deep breath and muttered the words: 'My ethnic origin is Asian, Black, White, Mixed, Other (Please Specify).'

The Warp

DR DAVID GOLDSTEIN CHECKED THE time on the till and saw that he still had ten more minutes to go. It had been dark outside for some time now, and the protesters who passed by the windows, with their placards glinting in the Christmas lights, gave the Games Workshop a strange, almost apocalyptic feeling, further heightened by the fact that David, who had still not lost his craving for nicotine, had now completely run out of gum.

'Excuse me but have you got any more Lizardmen?' said a boy with very thick glasses.

David shook his head. 'We're all out I'm afraid. But we've still got Elves, and Dwarves, you know everything else, we've got in. Even the Skaven.'

'But I really wanted Lizardmen.'

The boy looked pleadingly at David, and indeed his determination was so strong that the memory of the one remaining box located somewhere near the empty beer bottles pushed its way into David's mind, and then refused to leave it.

'Hang on a minute,' he said before darting off into the back room and returning a few seconds later with the last box. 'Okay so that's sixteen pounds then please.'

The boy got out his wallet and began to go through it, becoming more and more agitated as he did so.

'But I only have fifteen pounds!'

'I'm sorry but the recommended retail price is still sixteen pounds. Although all of the Elves are on sale. You could get two boxes for that, you—'

'But I don't want Elves! I want Lizardmen!'

The boy's eyes, which were magnified by his glasses, were now not only pleading but also helpless. David looked into them and then at the time on the till, which now showed that there were only five more minutes left to go. He took a deep breath and said, 'Okay. Fifteen pounds. But don't tell anyone okay?'

'Okay!'

David rang his purchase through the till, slipping in a pound coin that had become coated with the fluff and bits of sweets inside his pocket as he did so. Then he handed over the Lizardmen and followed the boy to the door, locking it behind him and turning off all of the lights in the display. He checked the time and saw that it was now half past five precisely. He took out his laptop and turned it on, and then went and stood in the middle of the room, lowered his head and hunched his shoulders, took another deep breath and muttered, 'My ethnic origin is Asian, Black, White, Mixed, Other (Please Specify)', while trying to visualise a red arc of light around his head.

Then he muttered, 'My national identity is English, Welsh, Scottish, Northern Irish, British, Other (Please Specify)', while trying to visualise a yellow arc of light around his throat.

Then he muttered, 'My gender is Male, Female, Other (Please Specify), Prefer not to Say', while trying to visualise a pink arc of light around his heart and lungs.

Then he muttered, 'My age range is 16–24, 25–34, 35–44, 45–54, 55–64, 65+', while trying to visualise a green arc of light around his stomach.

Then he muttered, 'My religion or belief is No Religion, Buddhist, Christian, Hindu, Jewish, Muslim, Sikh, Other (Please Specify), Prefer not to Say', while trying to visualise a purple arc of light around his genitals and anus.

Then he repeated each statement, and each attempt at visualisation, which was harder than he had anticipated, working up

137

from his genitals and anus and back towards his head. When he finished he took another deep breath and drew two arcs with his left hand, one that he visualised as orange, and one that he visualised as blue. Afterwards he made a forty-five-degree turn to the left, repeating the statements and the visualisations and the drawings in the air, and then another turn and then another until he was back where he started. And then he began again. Then he stood up straight, raised his head, pointed into the darkness of the window display and shouted, 'Look! A rainbow!'

In the background the telephone started to ring, but David ignored it. It switched to answer machine and a warbling voice inquired as to the availability of Dark Elves but not High Elves; but instead of going over and making a note of the details he began to shout out 'zero' and then 'one', over and over again in what seemed like a random order. Then the answer machine switched itself off. And then he went back over to his laptop where the little green light on his Gmail account was flashing.

David clicked on the Gmail window, where one unread message, with no subject header, had just appeared. He clicked on it, and a clipart drawing of cupid with a zero superimposed above his head opened out across the screen, accompanied by the message that it had been sent by Swopments. Then he clicked on another window, which showed a film of Kathy in the New College Media Hub. She was surrounded by computer screens and TV monitors, each of which showed him standing in the Games Workshop. Both he and Kathy looked into the image of each other, and then they both started chanting: 'A variety of things, a selection of items, an assortment of bags, jars and boxes.'

The little green light on David's Gmail account started flashing again, and then, still chanting and still listening to Kathy chanting, he clicked on the Gmail window. Now there was an unread email from someone called Hubber. The subject header said 'Bitch why won't you answer?' but when he opened it, it was blank. He kept on chanting with Kathy, however, watching his own face behind her and opening his emails, some of which were from someone called Swopments and contained clipart drawings of cupids with zeros superimposed above their heads, and some of which were from someone called Hubber and had the subject header 'Bitch why won't you answer?' but which, when he opened them, were blank. But he still went on and on chanting and checking his emails and looking into the image of Kathy until he wasn't sure quite what he was doing any more because he felt as if he was in some sort of trance.

Suddenly, David stopped, breathed deeply and closed his eyes. All of the various, useless items that he had recently packed up and taken back to his parents' house in West Bridgford now appeared to levitate in his mind. They were floating through a world of stars and fractals not dissimilar to the cover of either his or Paul's *The Kaosphere*, before finally landing on the clipart drawing of cupid with a zero superimposed above his head. Keeping his eyes closed he said, 'It is our will to utilise the Internet, both as a psycho-spiritual metaphor and a psychological-religious-political vehicle, through which to attain gnosis and thus transmit our sigilised erotic, philiac, ludic, agapean, pragmatic and philanthropic desires.' And the sound of Kathy, saying the same thing in the Media Hub, came back to him.

David opened his eyes and both he and Kathy looked into the image of each other. There was a pause, and then they both started to shout out 'zero' and then 'one' again, and again, in what appeared to be a random order that was nonetheless slightly different to the random order that had come before. After a while he started to record the chanting, and then he and Kathy stopped. He also pressed 'stop' on the recording and saved it as an MP3. Then he emailed the MP3 to his entire address book. Then he emailed an apology to his entire address book with the subject header 'Eek! My account's been hacked!' Then he took a deep breath and removed his Stop the War Coalition badge, revealing the Games Workshop logo, and waved it in front of his laptop. Then he turned off his laptop, and sat down on the floor ...

David remained there for some time, with pictures of all his various, useless items, the world of stars and fractals and the clipart drawing of cupid with a zero superimposed above his head still flashing, periodically, whenever he closed his eyes. Outside he could hear the sound of slurred voices, drunk on the spiced apple wine that they had recently started selling at the German Market; and on top of them the voices of the protestors discussing which pub to go to, and then finally deciding on Ye Olde Salutation Inn (or the Salutation Inn, as it was more widely known, or The Sal if you were local) . . .

David stood up, went into the backroom and opened the last bottle of beer that he could still see, hiding, amongst the empties. He downed it in pretty much one go and then went through his wallet, counting out his loose change and realising with some satisfaction that there was exactly the right amount for ten cigarettes. Then he put on his jacket, walked back out into the shop and, ignoring the crash that came from behind him, entered into the beginnings of the cold, dark night.

The Rite of Online Love

THIS IS A RITE FOR creating and attaining love via electronic sigil transmission. It utilises a pre-existing vector (in this case sections of the Evening Post Classified Advertisements, specifically Swop Shop and Family Announcements) while repurposing three, simultaneously existing physical sites (the Evening Post Classifieds office, the New College Media Hub and the Games Workshop), and therefore requires three participants, preferably of two or more genders, to complete it. During the Rite these participants should be known only by their magikal names of Swopments, Hubber and the Almighty Wizard GaWo.

STATEMENT OF INTENT:
It is our will to utilise the Internet, both as a psycho-spiritual metaphor and a psychological-religious-political vehicle, through which to attain gnosis and thus transmit our sigilised erotic, philiac, ludic, agapean, pragmatic and philanthropic desires.

RITE:
1. Open with the Unequal Opportunities Rite.
2. All participants to count to 0101, using binary numbers (0101 being equal to five and five referring to the Law of Fives previously summarised in relation to the Principia Discordia).

3. Swopments to email the erotic, philiac, ludic, agapean, pragmatic and philanthropic sigil to the Almighty Wizard GaWo that is the cupid-angel hybrid.
4. The Almighty Wizard GaWo to Skype Hubber, and then repeat the words, 'A variety of things, a selection of items, an assortment of bags, jars and boxes.'
5. Hubber to email a blank email to Swopments with the subject header, 'Answer my emails bitch!' followed by a blank email to the Almighty Wizard GaWo with the subject header, 'Bitch, why won't you answer?'
6. All participants to repeat these actions until a state of gnosis has been achieved.
7. All participants to visualise an assortment of bags, jars and boxes descending through cyberspace and landing on the cupid-angel hybrid. When they land say the Statement of Intent.
8. All participants to count backwards to 0101, using binary numbers.
9. All participants to re-perform step eight as an electronic file and then email it to everyone in their address books, immediately followed by an apology with the subject header, 'Eek! My account's been hacked!'
10. The Almighty Wizard GaWo to end the Rite through the usual banishing, in this case by repurposing his Stop the War Coalition badge as an evil eye, and passing it over his laptop.

Dave

DAVE WRAPPED THE FINAL PIECE of hazard tape around the re-collapsed shelving unit, and then lit a cigarette. It was not only his first of the morning but also his first for a very long time, and accordingly it gave him a slight but pleasant rush. The floor around him was still covered in Warhammer figures, as well as bits of broken wood and a few tiny pieces of safety glass, all of which still needed to be swept up – but he didn't feel any sense of urgency about it.

Instead he went over to the till, clicked out of the orders screen and onto the Internet, which he wasn't really meant to do at work, but which, as his laptop had already been infected with some sort of virus, he did anyway. Then he typed 'www.gmail. com' into the navigation bar, and then 'sameolddave' into the username box and then 'kiddish!' into the password box beneath it. He saw that he had one new email with the subject header 'puja', and was just about to click on it when a box of Lizardmen bumped down in front of him.

'Just these please,' said a boy who, judging by the little bits of tissue attached to his chin, had only recently started shaving.

'Okay that's sixteen pounds then.'

'But I've only got fifteen.'

Dave stubbed out his cigarette, and then immediately realised that he'd done so on Paul's copy of *The Kaosphere*. He brushed the ash onto the floor and said, 'Well I'm sorry but the recommended retail price is still sixteen pounds.'

The boy with the little bits of tissue attached to his chin pointed to the boy with very thick glasses, who was waiting, shamefacedly, behind him.

'But he said that you sell them for fifteen.'

Dave looked at the little burnt hole in the centre of *The Kaosphere*, then lit another cigarette, while visualising an achromatic arc encircling his heart and lungs. He glared at the boy with the very thick glasses and said, 'Then he needs to keep his mouth shut.'

'So I can't have them for fifteen then?'

'No. No, you can't.'

'But that's not fair!'

'No, it isn't. It's entirely random.'

'Fuck you!' said the boy with the bits of tissue attached to his chin, who then ran out of the shop.

The boy with the very thick glasses stood there looking scared, and then a second later he ran out after him. Dave laughed and clicked on 'puja':

Dear Dave,

I've been thinking about your experiment. Why don't you write it up as a paper, and then submit it to a proper journal? Professor Woźniak is always telling everyone about your work on belief and how brilliant it is – you really should do something with it.

Also, I know that we've missed Diwali but if you're still interested in all things Hindu then my parents are having a puja for my cousin's baby. It's in Leicester, obviously, but if we book in advance we can get cheap tickets.

Let me know if you fancy crossing cultural identities any time soon,

Meg X

Dave stared at the screen, thinking as he did so that if he hadn't been the Games Workshop Manager, or a doctor of theology and religious studies/geography, meaning had he been an entirely different type of man, then he would have punched the air. Instead, he reached for his phone, but Paul walked in before he could go any further.

'What's all, um, what's all, um, all this then?' Paul said nervously, looking at the various bits and pieces of debris on the floor.

'Don't worry I've got someone coming to fix it coming in tomorrow.'

'But you're, um, you're not in tomorrow.'

Dave put his phone back in his pocket, and then looked at Paul, who he now decided should really try to leave his comfort zone. He took a drag of his second cigarette, and said, 'So? I'm sure that you can handle it.'

'But I, um, I don't want to.'

'But you have to. Solidarity, mate, solidarity.'

Dave took another drag and then, remembering Paul's now defaced copy of *The Kaosphere*, covered it up with a pile of invoices. As he was doing so another boy came up to the counter, this time with a sticking plaster, only half covering a boil on his neck.

'How much are those?' he asked, pointing at the Lizardmen.

Dave picked up the box, examined it carefully, and put it down again. 'Nothing. They're free.'

The boy looked up at him with his mouth a little bit open. 'You sure?'

'No. So you better make the most of it before I change my mind.'

Dave handed over the box, which the boy held, tentatively, for a minute, before bolting out the shop. Then he laughed, took another drag and stubbed out his second cigarette on one of the invoices. He turned to Paul and said, 'So Paul. The Kaosphere. I was hoping that you could enlighten me.'

'Pardon?'

'The Kaosphere. How would you define it?'

'Oh, um, okay, yeah ... Well it's a kind of, um, a kind of occult anti-system in which eight arrows representing, um, representing all possibilities, and one arrow, representing the, um, the single, certain road of Law—'

'Excuse me but have you got any more Lizardmen?'

Another boy, this time with eczema, now stood before them.

'No, we're all out I'm afraid,' said Dave. 'Although we have just had a new delivery of Skaven.'

'And do they cost the same?'

'No. The smallest boxes of Skaven start at 250 pounds.'

'What?' said Paul.

'That seems like a lot. How about Orks?'

'I'm afraid that the Orks are beyond price. In fact, the Orks—'

'The Orks are sixteen pounds!' spluttered Paul.

Dave burst out laughing, and then, because he was no longer used to smoking, also burst out coughing, which gave Paul an excuse to take over and ring the box of Orks through the till. He waited until the boy had left, and then, as soon as they were alone, he turned to Dave and said, 'You know if anyone from the, um, from the, um, the management—'

'But I am the management.'

'I meant *senior* management. If any of them, um, if any of them heard about this—'

'This?'

'Yes *this*. Giving stuff away. Making up silly prices. Intimidating the, um, customers—'

'I was hardly intimidating them.'

'Then you'd be out of a job. You know there's plenty of, um, people who'd give their right arm to work here.'

'But ...' But Dave opted to bite his tongue rather than point out that, by people, Paul meant teenage boys, and then said, 'You know, maybe I *should* resign.'

Paul looked at the broken display unit and then back at him aghast. 'But what else could you, um, do?'

Meg

MEG TOOK OFF HER RUCKSACK, removed her camera and entered the City of Caves. She already knew each of the wall texts off by heart, including the panel that now rose out of the darkness. It informed her, the visitor, that the city of Nottingham had once been known as Tigguo Cobauc, which in ye olde English meant 'place of caves', just as Kathy had once informed her, the tourist, that Tora Bora meant 'black cave' in Pashto. Mentally Meg compared the words 'Tiggo Cobauc', as the panel depicted them now, meaning a typeface that resembled handwriting, with what she knew of Pashto, meaning squiggles and diamonds; and then she compared them both, unfavorably, to Kannada.

She walked down a narrow flight of stairs and into a series of sandstone caves that, unlike the limestone caves that lay beneath the mountains of Afghanistan, lay beneath the Broadmarsh Shopping Centre. Then she wove her way through the dim recreations of 'Underground Brewing', 'Underground Storage' and 'Air Raid Shelters', each of which (or so the wall texts stated) had once been really real, while every now and then bits of grit, caused by the rumble of overhead traffic, fell onto her newly shorn head.

After a minute or so, she came to 'Underground Tannery', which like the neighbouring 'Underground Cess Pit', utilised a degree of poetic licence in terms of cave curation. Whereas the previous areas aimed for authenticity, the cess pit was lit by fluorescent green bulbs, while the tannery was decorated in a style not dissimilar to that of a horror movie, with animal skulls and rags. Meg reread the panel, which informed her, the anthropologist, that the tannery had once produced 'boots, shoes, gloves and belts for military use, as well as scabbards, quivers, helmets, armour and shields', and then examined the board showing different tanning samples, all of which reminded her of the pile of her own hair on the floor of her own room, which was no longer very tidy.

Meg set up her camera, crouched down and looked out through the viewfinder, where she saw that a drawing of a penis was framed between the calfskin and the pigskin samples on the wall. It had been made with a black marker pen, and there was a line of dots arcing out of the top of it, which was then cut off by one of the leather squares. She wondered how many years it would take before the drawing ceased to be a sign of vandalism, and instead became a fertility symbol, reframed and intellectualised in numerous unread books ...

There was a buzz inside Meg's pocket. She took out her phone and saw that she had a text message, and then put it back again without reading what it said. Then she took some pictures of the skins and of the skulls, some of which were arranged on tree stumps, and some of which were piled up on the floor. Then, when she had finished, she moved on to the air raid shelter, where a picture of Winston Churchill had been hung above a camp bed half covered with an army blanket. She sat down on the bench opposite and thought about how, now that all the different bits of her body had come back together again, she no longer needed her hair, but that her ears, which were cold, wanted something else to cover them ...

After a while Meg stood up again and moved on to 'Underground Living'. This time she, the viewer, had to stand along a narrow pathway and twist round so as to see into each of the different sections of the cave. Different pieces of furniture had been arranged in each one, so that each resembled a different room. A series of cardboard rats had been arranged in the first 'kitchen cave', as well as a cardboard cat, while another, uncaptioned cave was filled with cardboard chickens. For a moment she wondered whether or not the cardboard chickens laid cardboard eggs; and then whether or not she should read her text message; and then whether or not it was finally time to accept the fact that she would never be daring or poetic or romantic, and that Dr David Goldstein, who had, at one point, been the Cross-Cultural Identities Research Group convener, was someone she could quite easily fit in with ...

Meg kept on walking, her shoes making a different type of scrunching sound depending on whether she stood on sand or gravel, until she was back at the City of Caves reception. She blinked, and then, as her eyes gradually became accustomed to the light, took in the various guidebooks, all of which she had already read. There was also a new display of lamps and coasters made from rocks arranged inside a mirrored cabinet. She looked into the cabinet and examined the space that had once been her hair ...

Meg left the City of Caves and wandered out into the Broadmarsh Shopping Centre. The only other people she could see were a couple and their baby, who were stood in front of the toilets. The man muttered something and the woman gripped the handles of the pushchair, gritted her teeth and said, 'I'm stuck at home all day, I've put on weight, and I just don't feel like it, alright?' And then the baby started crying.

Meg walked past them, up the escalator and out onto the street. Even though Christmas was still a week away, the sales had already started. She walked past dozens of shops filled with signs saying, 'Up to 30 per cent off', and 'Up to 50 per cent off' and 'Up to 70 per cent off', while her shoes made a different type of sound depending on whether she stood on the slush-covered paving stones or the slush-covered remnants of placards. She stepped over a piece of paper that said, 'Stop the War', and then went into a shop that said, 'Buy One Get the Second One Free', and selected a red bobble-hat and a blue beret because they couldn't both turn against her.

Meg paid for her hats and carried on walking, past the beginnings of the sales and the remnants of the protests, and up into the Market Square. She paused in front of one of the stalls, and examined the very chic children's toys that were laid out on a felt cloth in front of her, before selecting a miniature train. Then she handed it, and her money, over to the stall owner, thinking that it would make a suitable gift for Denesh, which was the name of her new first cousin once removed. And then she reached for her phone.

Stan

STAN WALKED UP THROUGH THE Market Square. He was carrying
a large coil of German sausages, which he had bought on account
of their being not dissimilar to Polish sausages, which were one of
the few things about the old country that he missed. It had only
just stopped raining, and as he turned the corner into Friar Lane
he almost slipped on the remnants of an abandoned placard. He
stopped, steadied himself and looked down at the slogan – 'Bring
Our Boys Home' – that was slicked to the pavement in front of him.

Stan shook his head and carried on walking until he reached
the Games Workshop, and then stopped again, wondering quite
what he should do with the sausages. Briefly he considered putting them down his trousers, but then thought better of it, and
a moment later looped them over his belt instead. He entered
the shop and strolled over to Paul, who was sitting behind the
till, painting a miniature dragon. Stan coughed loudly and Paul
looked up, taking in the sausages, and then his 'In Case of Emergency Break *Dance*' tee-shirt. Stan smiled at Paul, pointed at the
hazard tape and said, 'Matchie, matchie.'

Paul put down the paintbrush, and then passed his hand
across his mouth, inadvertently covering it with a large streak of
red enamel.

'Oh, um, yes. I see what you mean.'

'You work for Dave, yes?'

'Well sort of yes. I mean I actually work for the Games Workshop, but yes Dave's the, um, manager, but he's not actually working today so—'

'Dave thinks my tee-shirt very funny.'

'Yes, I'm sure he does, but I – it's his day off and I'm actually the assistant manager—'

'So you are not the manager.'

Paul blushed and stood up rather awkwardly. Then he walked Stan over towards the display unit and said, 'Okay, so this time it's the other side that's broken.'

'More mice people?'

'Yes, and so if you don't mind fixing it back onto the wall again I've got a few um bits and pieces to be getting on with.'

Paul turned back towards the counter, while Stan began to unwind the string of sausages from around his waist. Then, as soon as he had finished untangling them, he grabbed hold of Paul's retreating shoulder and pressed the sausages against his chest.

'You look after for me, yes?'

'Um . . .'

Reluctantly, Paul took the sausages and stashed them beside Dave's laptop underneath the till, while Stan began to rummage in his toolbox until he found a bag of nails. He inserted one of them between his lips and said, 'Sausages go well with beer, yes?' And then, when no answer was forthcoming, 'It is good to have the beer, yes?'

But Paul's attention was already taken up with a customer.

'That's sixteen pounds then please.'

'Sixteen? But yesterday they were free.'

'Well I'm sorry but the, um, the recommended retail price is still sixteen pounds.'

'Sixteen pounds is too much,' bellowed Stan from the window. 'You get cheap doll, very cheap, down Sneinton Market.'

'They're not dolls' – Paul's voice took on a prissy tone – 'they're miniatures.'

Stan snorted. He began to hammer one of the nails into one of the boards, and as he hit it, squarely on the head, he thought firstly about how much he liked Dave – whose awkwardness seemed like more of a trope, or form of politeness even, than genuine unease – and then about how best to have some fun with Paul, who was boring. He watched as Paul handed over one of the boxes, and then waited for the boy who had bought them to make his way towards the exit. Then, just as he was passing by, he gave a vigorous tug to the only part of the shelving unit that was still attached to the wall. The board crashed down onto the floor and the boy jumped back, nearly upsetting the other, only recently mended display, while Paul cowered meekly behind him. Stan laughed loudly, and then began to hammer in another nail. After a while he said, 'I would like the beer now yes.'

'Excuse me?'

'Dave always gives me the beer. I work cheap. So I get the beer.'

Paul looked unsure but nevertheless put down his paints and disappeared out the back. A minute later he returned holding a dusty bottle which Stan took from him, and then uncapped using the claw end of his hammer. Straight away he took a swig and said, 'I do not mind if you also have the beer Paul. You must not stand on the ceremonies.'

Paul nodded but did not take a beer. Stan banged in another row of nails and said, 'Paul I have feeling that one day it will be you, not Dave, who is manager.'

Paul blinked very slowly. 'Well, I mean, Dave would have to, um, resign first. Or get fired, or else I mean I suppose that they could always bring in some sort of, um, restructuring and—'

Stan put his hammer back in the toolbox, went over to the counter and slapped Paul on the shoulder. Then he picked up the half-painted figure in front of him, inadvertently covering his fingers in red. He turned it slowly and, looking at Paul, said, 'Look, your lizard is bleeding.'

'It's not a lizard, it's a dragon.'

'Ah yes,' and Stanisław laughed loudly so that the gold teeth at the back of his mouth now showed. 'Ah yes Paul, the dragon doll.'

153

Kathy

KATHY STARED, HARD, AT ONE of the many computer screens in the New College Media Hub. She felt sick, and also hungry, because having felt permanently sick ever since she saw the video of Eoin, she hadn't really been eating, and this meant that she'd finally reached a point where the sickness and the hunger just spiralled round and round inside her, not quite filling up the empty space. Then she typed 'www.hotmail.com' into the navigation bar, and then her email, and then her password, and then she deleted all of the unread messages from journalists and trolls, and then she stared at the no new or unread messages that failed to fill her unfillable inbox, before clicking onto 'Astro Alerts', where the daily horoscope for Cancer read:

Today's trine between Neptune in your ninth house and the Scorpio moon will do much to soften the crab's hard shell. Life will be a lot easier when you've made certain pressing decisions; just remember, every interaction holds the promise of deep personal connection and fulfilment.

Except that she couldn't even remember what it felt like to connect, or to be fulfilled anymore, because she couldn't even remember Eoin anymore – only that he had left her and that nothing else could fill the space. She remembered what the photographs of him looked like obviously, all of which were by their nature flat and partial, and she would have remembered the fragments of his voice had the last voicemail message that he left her not been automatically deleted – but as for the man himself? The Internet had erased her hope, and this hope, she now realised, had been indistinguishable from her love. And then she cracked her knuckles, so that they made a sound like her spine breaking, and typed in the following:

Dear Eoin,
    Margaret is ill in hospital. If you ring the Queen's Medical Centre and ask for Stroke Recovery they'll put you through.
    Kathy

Which translated as:

I am dead, blind, implicit – or even nothing.

Kathy pressed 'send', and then watched as the 'compose' screen morphed into the 'your message has been sent' screen and then back into the 'inbox' screen with no new or unread messages. Then she signed out of her Hotmail account, closed Astro Alerts, and opened a new blank Word document, because she had decided to apply for a place at a film school that was not in Nottingham, which, although it didn't necessarily mean moving forward, would at least mean moving away.

Kathy started typing into the new blank Word document, detailing how and why she met the course criteria. Out of the corner of her eye she could see Jackson approaching her desk, and then, as soon as he drew level with it, he stopped and smiled.

'So Kathy, I hear that you're thinking of making an application to film school?'

'Yes I'm doing it now actually.'

'Well if you need a reference . . .?'

She typed the words, 'I am passionate about all aspects of film production' into the Word document.

155

'Yes, that would be great.'

'Or if you need anyone to look over it for you . . .?'

She typed the words, 'I would relish the opportunity to continue my studies in a critically engaged and supportive environment'.

'Yes that would be great.'

Jackson checked his watch.

'Well the session finishes in five minutes. Why don't we go for a coffee?'

Kathy checked her phone.

'I've got to meet my mum.'

'Well another time then?'

'Sure.'

Kathy adjusted her baseball cap to show that the conversation had ended and Jackson walked away. Then she deleted all of the words, and stared at the sick, hungry space. She still didn't know if Eoin had made it into the actual newspapers yet, but she was pretty sure that everyone, including Jackson, including her friends, including her parents, must just know; just as she was pretty sure that their response to it wouldn't be to offer her the relief that would come from being the victim of their anger, their rage even, but the slow, cold ice of pity . . .

Kathy closed the new blank Word document without saving. She zipped up her big white puffa jacket so that her body, like her face, became invisible, and then she left New College. She could see a newsagents up ahead, but as soon as she got near enough to read the headlines she pulled her hood up over her baseball cap and shut her eyes. And then she began to run. And kept on running, away from New College, and the newsagents, and towards her mother, whose love and familiarity she wanted but whose unspoken knowledge and pity she feared. She knew that she must be stepping on every crack and every line but what did that matter when every part of her was already broken? When the someone, somewhere, who was punishing her, had already stuck so many pins into their little Kathy-shaped doll that there wasn't any room for any more?

Kathy opened her eyes just as a woman carrying a poinsettia stepped out of a nearby doorway. Kathy swerved, skidding on the remainder of a placard stuck to one of the concrete slabs. She tried to stop herself but there was nothing to grab onto except the poinsettia, which she now knocked out of the woman's hands, smashing it as she fell. Then she lay on the wet, white ground, not entirely comprehending what had happened to her, while a small crowd of people began to gather. Gradually she saw that there was a piece of terracotta lodged in her palm, which was bleeding, and then that her jacket was torn, and that the duck down feathers that had filled it, and which were now sticking to her hair, were almost the same type of white as the snow.

Kathy looked up at the sky and then down at the ground and she saw that there was white snow, and red blood and bits of broken pottery; and a torn piece of paper that said 'Number One Terrorist'; and flowers, petals, on her hands, her face, her body, which must have been symbolic of something.

Margaret

MARGARET FELT VERY SAD AND very lonely and very scared, but also very determined not to let it show. Instead she sat, very still, in her metal-framed hospital bed and grappled with her rosary. She was aware of how, when she had first arrived, she wouldn't even have been able to make a fist with which to hold the beads, but that now she could place the chain within the palm of her weaker hand, and then pull it through with her stronger one. She was still some way off being able either to hoover, wash up, make tea, arrange the flowers or send an email, but at least she now had the tools with which to will them into happening.

Dear Holy Mother, said Margaret, in silence, Dear Holy Virgin, Dear Our Lady of Sorrows, Grace, Light, Mercy, etc., please help me, and him, and them to get through this, just as I have gotten through everything else that God, in his infinite wisdom, has thrown at me. And then she pulled the first bead into the centre of her palm and began on her first Our Father. And as she prayed she looked at the Our Lady-shaped bottle of water stood on the side, the height, colour and painted expression of which was almost identical to the statuette at home. And then she tugged the chain with her stronger hand, and held a new bead in the palm of her weaker one and thought about how, if Albertina kept on like this, then she might, just possibly, be allowed to *assist* her with the flowers …

'Looks like you've got a visitor Margaret,' said Lucy, and Margaret's right eye flickered.

Sure enough, there was another black lady stood behind her, only instead of a white cotton uniform, she was wearing a waxed cotton dress. Margaret watched as Lucy inspected the clipboard attached to the end of the bed, and then smiled her nice smile, while Blessings pulled out one of the chairs and arranged her frills upon it.

'And how are you doing today?' said Lucy.

'Much better thank you. I should be able to go home soon don't you think?'

Lucy wrote something on the clipboard, while Blessings took Margaret's weaker hand, and thus her rosary beads in hers. 'Yes. But we want to make sure that you're absolutely fighting fit first,' said Lucy, still smiling.

'We had Father Jonathan say a mass for a speedy recovery,' said Blessings, smiling also.

'But I do want to go home soon,' said Margaret, looking from one nice black lady to the other. 'I want to be home by Christmas.'

Lucy and Blessings smiled at each other, while Margaret's right eye flickered and then stopped. She looked from Lucy to Blessings again, and said, 'You know you two could almost be sisters.'

Lucy and Blessings both laughed.

'But I am old enough to be her mother. And I am fatter too,' said Blessings.

'Oh no Blessings not at all, you're a fine figure of a woman.'

Blessings and Lucy smiled at each other again as Lucy picked up one of the ordinary hospital pillows and plumped it up to make it poufy. Then she placed it, and another type of pillow made from foam, behind Margaret's back, and said goodbye. Blessings then pulled her chair even closer to the bed and, taking hold of Margaret's other hand, so that she now held both of them between her bigger, darker ones, she began to talk about St Flannan's. And as Margaret listened to the soothing pitter-patter of these very minor gossips, she felt the strength of her fear, as well as her hatred, subsiding . . .

'Pray for the mourner,' she said sadly.

'I'm sorry Margaret?'

'It's from a hymn. Hail Queen of Heaven. I used to sing it when I was a girl.'

'Hail Queen of Heaven? Would you like me to ask Father Jonathan to include it? Next time we have a mass said?'

'Oh no. And I won't need another mass. I'm nearly well again.' Margaret removed her hearing aid and placed it beside her Bible, and then, in a frail attempt to change the subject, 'And do you sing the same songs in Malawi?'

'Oh no. It's very different. For a start we have drums instead of an organ, and everybody dances.'

'In church?'

'Yes. We dance in the spirit.'

'Oh ... Well I suppose if the priests don't mind.' Margaret tried to smile, although the thought of drumming and dancing throughout the mass didn't seem quite right to her, mainly because she could not imagine, and indeed did not want to imagine, any such thing at St Flannan's, and then, 'And what about the animals? Do they join in as well?'

'The animals?'

'I don't know ... I just thought that ...'

'Yes?'

'You know Eoin always wanted a puppy. But it was difficult you see. Especially after my daughter died. I didn't have much money, or a garden ...'

They both sat quietly for a minute. The noise of the television in the next cubicle drifted through and mingled with the sound of a trolley being wheeled along the corridor. Margaret sighed and said, 'Will you say the rosary with me Blessings?'

'Yes Margaret. Yes of course.'

Blessings reached inside her purse for her own set of beads, and then both she and Margaret bowed their heads. They murmured their way through the first Our Father, and then the first Hail Mary, and then, just as they were about to start on their second, another, younger voice cut across them, saying, 'There's a call for you Margaret.'

Margaret raised her head and saw that Lucy was back at the end of the bed, but that this time she was holding a telephone.

'For me?'

'I can tell him to ring back later if you'd like?'

'No, no it's alright.'

Lucy squeezed in around the side of the bed and handed her the receiver.

'Hello. Nottingham 923 ...' said Margaret, but then stopped, remembering that she wasn't at home, and listened instead to the sound of static refilling her aging ears. 'Hello?' She tried and failed to tap the speaking end. 'Hello? Hello?'

'Nana it's—'

She felt the strain in her frozen hands, as they attempted to grip the receiver, as tightly as possible, against her ear.

'Eoin? Eoin is that you?'

'Aye Nana. It's me. It's Eoin.'

Paddy

PADDY, WHO HAD ONCE BEEN Eoin O'Shea but was now just plain Paddy Nothing, looked up and the guard, who was also a soldier, caught his eye and nodded. Paddy nodded back at him and said, 'Goodbye then.'

Then he placed the old-fashioned telephone receiver back in its cradle and followed the guard to what was now his cell in Colchester Military Prison. He knew that being here, in D Company, was considerably better than being in the Military Customary Platoon, the majority of whom would soon be sent on to Pentonville, but considerably worse than being in A Company, all of whom would eventually be returned to their regiments as opposed to being dishonourably discharged.

Paddy entered his cell, which was also a kind of dormitory and looked up at the clock on the wall, where 1300 flashed in broken red. Lock-down was nine hours away, but because he was always tired, he lay down and shut his eyes. In Iraq, he had hated the night-times the most, at first because of the constant but invisible mortar fire, and then because of the memory of it, which slithered inside his dreams. Now, however, he saw the darkness as a kind of safety blanket, underneath which he felt nothing except the absence of fear, or indeed any other emotion . . .

'But this isn't really a prison,' said a man's voice.

'But we're locked up,' said another, 'so how can it not be?'

Paddy balled his hands into fists and pushed them into his eye sockets, but still the numbers kept on thrusting, as did the voices ...

'Paddy?' said a third, slightly softer voice that sounded very close to him, and then, 'So did you do it Paddy?'

Finally, Paddy opened his eyes. He looked through the boy leaning over him and out of the window, which, apart from the clock, was the only interruption on the otherwise plain, institutionalised walls. The sky was grey with clouds, which meant that the new red-brick building on the other side of the quad appeared to seep into the ground in front of it, while the barbed wire curled and spiked around the twigs' edges as though it too were an extension of the trees. It was the same as every other view, he thought ruefully, the only difference being that sometimes there was earth or sand instead of tarmac, and that sometimes the weather had burnt instead of chilled him. He rolled over to face the boy who was just a boy and said, 'I'm not sure.'

The boy opened his mouth, but before he could respond the sound of footsteps marching in unison with one another, reverberated through the dormitory's walls. It grew louder as it neared them, and then just as quickly died away.

'Time to get going,' said the first man.

'No rest for the wicked,' said the second.

Reluctantly, Paddy got up and followed them outside. When they reached the quad they joined the other men and made a circle, standing with their legs apart and their hands behind their backs. In the centre a mechanic, who was also a soldier, began to demonstrate just what could and could not be done with an engine, removing its different components and hammering them into shape. There was something compelling, meditative even, about the way in which each piece either twisted apart or slotted together, before finally making the deep metallic purr that proved that it was sound.

'So now I want to see you do it.'

The circle broke into lines and marched towards the shelter opposite, then picked up the photocopied instruction sheets.

Paddy looked at his and straight away it made sense, in the same precise, practical way that anything precise and practical always did. He was good with his hands, that was what his Nana said, and then, when they got together, Kathy had said it too – although she had meant to imply something different. He was about to reach for the spanner, but then noticed the man beside him, who was staring.

'You alright?' said Paddy.

He stared back, with the same take-no-shit-never stare that he had learned, pretty early on, was the only type of stare to give if you didn't want to get a kicking, but the man's gaze didn't waver. He was holding the information sheet so tightly that it looked as though it were about to tear, and because of this his knuckles had completely drained of colour.

'I said, "Are. You. All. Right",' Paddy repeated.

He waited for the man to either look away or go for him, and braced himself in preparation for the latter – except that the man just kept staring, and then eventually blurted out, 'I don't understand it.' And then, 'And I'm old.'

In response there was silence, from Paddy and from all the other prisoners, who had once been soldiers, and who likewise pretended not to hear. A moment or so passed, and then Paddy eased the sheet out from between his fingers, and laid it on the workbench. He almost felt a stab of compassion, but dodged it before it could cut into him, because by now he knew that it was rules that saved you and not any so-called friendships; and this being the path via which he'd learned to like, or at least escape from, what had once been his career, he had no wish to deviate from it. Rather he waited until he was sure that none of the other prisoners were looking at them, and then said quietly: 'C'mon, how old are you? Thirty?'

'But I signed up when I was sixteen,' said the man, in the same way one might have said that he had just turned a hundred. 'This is all I can do. Only I can't.'

Paddy looked through the man who had been a man since being a boy, and at the view that was the same as any other, and which was now being obscured by rain. He could see the army chaplain, who was also a civilian chaplain, and seeing him the two-faced chaplain waved. Paddy ignored him, and then reached for the spanner, the sharp part of the open end catching the edge of his palm as he did so. For the first time, he looked down and there was grease and blood on his hands.

Occupational Therapy

MARGARET SAT ON THE EDGE of the settee with her right hand held out in front of her as though she were about to perform a karate chop. Even holding this position for a very short time was painful, a situation that was greatly exacerbated by the dust that had already begun to gather across the top of the mantelpiece opposite.

'Okay so first of all Margie—'

'It's Margaret. I was baptised Margaret and Margaret is what I've always been called,' said Margaret sharply.

'Okay so first of all *Margaret*,' and the occupational therapist smiled so that her straight, white teeth shone against her brown winter-sun complexion, 'what I want you to do is this.' She bent her own hand so that the fingers made a horizontal line. 'Some of my patients say that it helps to imagine the top of a little table.'

Slowly and painfully Margaret bent her hand until it resembled the occupational therapist's hand, and tried to hold the position. She could see, out of the corner of her eye, that her new 2005 calendar was hanging a little lower than it should be, and that this made it seem as though the blue statuette was standing, not in front of 'Sunset over Santorini', as the caption underneath the photograph stated, but floating over a raging sea of flames.

'I don't know if it's meant to be the end times or the assumption,' said Margaret, and then looked back at her crooked hands.

'Well that seems a little bit extreme to me *Margaret*, although some of my patients do say that it hurts to begin with. Anyway, now that we've got our nice flat little table top I want you to pull up your fingers up like this,' and this time the occupational therapist bent the top of her knuckles back, 'and try to imagine a little claw.'

Slowly and painfully Margaret bent the top of her knuckles back until they resembled the top of the occupational therapist's knuckles.

'That's right *Margaret*. And now I want to see you do it five more times.'

Margaret pressed her lips together and began to bend her fingers back into the little tabletop position, and then, after what seemed like an eternity had passed, back into the little claw position, and then she let both her hands drop into her lap, scowled and said, 'But how is this going to help with Christmas dinner?'

'With *Christmas* dinner Margaret? In January? Now I seem to remember that when we made our list—'

'But I want to make sure that Eoin gets a Christmas dinner. He wasn't allowed to have one you see.'

'He wasn't *allowed*?'

'Yes. In Colchester. He had to stay there over Christmas, but next month he'll be home.'

Margaret clutched her weaker hand with her stronger one and then dug her nails into it. She had lived, for the entirety of the last week, within a tumult of emotion: at first relief that Eoin was safe from the Muslims, but then worry that Eoin was not safe from the army, and then guilt for what she herself must have done, or failed to do, to cause this unsafe situation now. She thought about Eoin, after his mother had died, and how frightened and withdrawn he had been when he had first come to live with her. She had done what she could, of course, and worked evenings and weekends to support him. But that meant that she hadn't always been there. And that meant that both of them had all too often been alone. If only she had loved harder, loved better. If only, if only. She looked back at the occupational therapist and down at her own little clawing hand, and then, before the occupational therapist had time to press her for a more detailed explanation, said, 'And have you always lived in Nottingham, err . . .?'

'Aida. Yes, yes I have actually.'

Margaret paused and considered the name, and likewise the skin tone, which was probably English, but possibly worse.

'But what about your parents, *Aida*?'

'Same. I can never decide if that's because we're a very happy family or a very lazy family or—'

'But what about your grandparents, *Aida*?'

'My grandparents?'

'Yes, are they English, or . . .?'

'Or?' But Margaret only flickered at her until Aida was forced to continue, 'Well, err, yes, although my dad's mum, she's from Donegal – but this is an awful lot of questions Margaret? I mean why? Why do you ask?'

Margaret pressed her lips together, and then tried and failed to remove her hearing aid, and then tried and failed to remember all the reasons why she was angry and had a right to be angry and how they had dug into and then clung onto her since birth; and yet they now appeared to be eluding her, just as God was, temporarily, eluding her even though she knew that He still existed, somewhere up above the crosses kept in boxes and the raging sea of flames.

'Look, why don't I put the kettle on and make us both a cup of tea, and then when we've both got our breath back I can show you some exercises to strengthen your wrists?' said Aida.

'But you're the – actually yes, yes a cup of tea would be very nice.'

Aida stood and made her way towards the kitchen. As she passed by the mantelpiece she stopped and picked up the statuette, turning it expertly in her neat brown hands.

'Excuse me!' said Margaret.

'Oh, oh silly me I am sorry,' said Aida, very quickly, and put it back upon the shelf. 'It's only – I mean it's just that it reminded me of school.'

'Of school?'

'Yes. There used to be a little statue like this in the chapel, and whenever you did something wrong – and everything there was always wrong, I mean it was a Catholic grammar school, so you can just imagine – well then you had to go and stand beside it. And the punishment was always the same one – a decade of the rosary while you thought about your sins.'

Death from a Thousand Cuts

DAVE STOOD IN HIS PARENTS' kitchen reading *Voodoo: A Beginner's Guide*, while at the same time slicing lemons for Meg's tea. Since they had been spending all their time together, they'd been at his parents' house a lot. Ideally, he would have been standing in the kitchen of his own place, except he didn't have his own place, and Meg didn't like her own place because of Matthew, whose behaviour, or so she claimed, had become particularly trying lately. He had just reached a particularly interesting section on the serpent god Danbala – who was syncretised with St Patrick, and which meant that the Haitians slaughtered a goat and went into a trance on St Patrick's Day rather than simply drinking too much and then falling over in the street – when, his attention having wandered from the chopping board, he inadvertently chopped his finger.

'Shit!' said Dave, as he caught sight of the blood, and then 'Ouch!' as his brain caught up with his eyes and the acid began to sting him.

'Let me see,' said Meg, and her hand encircled his wrist and twisted it, palm upwards towards her. 'I don't think you'll need a stitch or anything just—' and then, 'Shit!' as her eyes caught up with her brain and she realised that there was blood all over their things.

Dave followed her gaze, looking first of all at his own packet of cigarettes, and then at Meg's half-completed Waterstones application, and finally at the man plastered all over *The Times*. He was handsome, but also vulnerable-looking, due to the hint of softness still hovering round his jaw, or else maybe it was his bottom lip, which looked as though it had been caught mid-tremble, that made him seem so helpless. He reminded Dave of Rufus Sewell, or else some other hard-man-pretty-boy star, and his likeness to him, and so to Hollywood, was so arresting that one hardly noticed the broken flesh in the background, which, like everything else in the immediate vicinity, was now spotted red from his bleeding finger.

'Isn't that—'

'Yes,' said Meg, while reaching for a piece of kitchen roll. 'And he's in *The Mirror*, *The Sun*, even *The Guardian*.'

'I wonder if Kathy's seen it yet.'

'She must have done. It's been all over the Internet for days now.'

Meg tugged at one of the drawers underneath the hob until the broken runner finally jolted open, and a box of sticking plasters fell out onto the floor. She picked it up and handed it to him, and then moved her application form to the other, less cluttered end of the table. Although Dave already knew, because Meg had already told him, that the Free Ads was about to 'go digital', meaning that in spite of its antiquated content and antiquated readership, said readership could now input their bags of assorted items, by themselves, online, and meaning that by the end of next month Meg and Kathy's analogue skills would no longer be required, he couldn't help wondering if Waterstones was really the right place for someone with Meg's ambition, or at any rate relentlessness, to be going; and yet at the same time it had never occurred to him that this could merely be a stepping stone for her to someplace else.

'But don't you even want to try and apply for a research post?' he said, attempting to sop up some of the blood with his sleeve but actually just smearing it across a larger area. 'I mean even I just handed in my notice.'

'What?' She tried to push the broken drawer back in. 'You've just ...?'

'I've just, err, handed in my notice.'

'But what else will you do? I mean, have you contacted Professor Woźniak? Maybe he could get you something? Or-or—'

'Actually, I already know what I'm going to do. I'm going to start a blog. On magik – with an, err, "k".' And then, because he couldn't help himself, he smiled.

'A blog?' said Meg, uncertainly. 'A blog and . . .?'

'And nothing. A blog on magik. That's it.'

Ignoring Meg's all too obvious unease, Dave reopened his book and resumed the section on Danbala, making a mental note that he not only ruled the mind and the intellect, but also the cosmic equilibrium. He smiled again, and then without looking up he handed Meg her tea, a gesture that, however absent-minded, was nonetheless informed by an image of their combined futures in which he, a part-time house husband, part-time super-blogger, took care of these small chores.

'And have you got any of your hair left over? From when you cut it?' he said amiably, noting also that Danabla's wife, Ayida-Weddo, lived with him in the sky.

'I haven't got time for any more experiments Dave.' And then, as if for extra emphasis, she actually kicked the drawer so that the broken runner squealed. 'Unless of course you want to remove the hex on Kathy Flowers? I mean if ever anyone had a run of bad luck it's her.'

'Actually that's not such a bad idea.'

'For fuck's sake I was joking.'

Dave shut the book and turned to face her, but she had already given up on him, and was now jabbing her fingers into the very hot water in her cup. He felt that she was, in that moment, slipping from him, and that consequently he needed to make her understand that, although he had now found his calling, he still loved her, just as much as his blog – or the idea of it – and that it was simply that, now that their relationship, unlike the blog idea, was a reality, it was she and not the blog that could be asked to wait. He reached out, tentatively, towards her, laid one hand on her arm and said, 'Listen, Meg, you don't have to worry, I still—'

'But no Dave. No.'

Although just what it was that she was saying no to – the ritual, the hair or his presence generally – he could not be sure. So instead, he merely watched as, finally, she skewered the offending piece of lemon on her finger and held it out in front of him, accusingly.

Blood and Saltwater

KATHY LOOKED AROUND THE BROADWAY Cinema café-bar, which was the café-bar of Nottingham's only arthouse cinema, and therefore an appropriate place for an Access to Media lecturer and a documentary filmmaker to have chosen as a first date setting, and what she saw was hazy. She was about to get her period, which made everything seem even worse than usual, which meant eating even less than usual while crying even more than usual, and all of this – the sorrow and the hunger and the tears – meant that the wine, which she wasn't used to drinking, had made her very drunk very quickly.

She looked at the art students, and middle-aged art teachers and various other members of the bona fide middle classes sitting around her, and then back at Jackson, who was handsome. Not handsome in the same old-fashioned film star way that Eoin was handsome, obviously, or she would have noticed it sooner, but handsome in the kind of nice, soft way that would appeal to someone's mother ...

'Are you alright?' said Jackson, tilting his head to one side. 'Anyone would think that you'd never set foot in here before.'

'That's probably because I never have set foot in here before, or tasted wine before, or been out with a bona fide member of the middle classes before. I'm drunk on new experiences.'

174

Jackson laughed, as though what she had said was a joke, even though it was actually not a joke but true, and Kathy smiled and said, 'Although that also means that I'm a really cheap date.' And this time she laughed as well because this time it was a joke, while Jackson carried on laughing because he was full, and sure of himself as well as nice and soft, and so hadn't paused from his first lot of laughing before.

'So does that mean you do or don't want another glass of wine Miss Katherine?'

'Katherine?'

'Sorry. I was being stupid.'

'No you weren't.' She put down her wine glass, 'It's just that my real name is actually Katarzyna.'

'Kata – Katasss—'

'Katarzyna. It's the 'zy' sound that's difficult.' She pursed her full, pink lips, 'zy, zy.'

Jackson watched, and then pursed his thin ones.

'Zy?'

'That's right. Kat-ar-zy-na!'

'Kat-ar-zy-na.'

'Perfect.'

'Kat-ar-zy-na.' Jackson resumed laughing. 'You have a beautiful name. Kat-ar-zy-na. And much nicer than Kathy if you don't mind me saying.'

'I don't mind. In fact, I only changed it to try and fit in at school – not that it made any difference.'

Kathy took another sip of wine and smiled and then finished her wine and smiled and realised that Jackson was even nicer and softer and also slightly hazier than before, as well as having changed from mildly to very good looking. Jackson leaned over and brushed her hair out of her eyes, which in one sense seemed slightly naff, but in another like something that someone in a film would do and therefore charming.

'Kids can be so cruel,' he said, softly.

'Or indifferent. Or they can just stop answering your emails.'

'Your emails?'

'Umm ...'

Jackson took another sip of wine while Kathy went back to watching all of the other inhabitants of the Broadway Cinema café-bar in the same way that she might have done had she been watching the animals in a zoo. They all appeared to be so full of themselves, these bona fide middle-class people, and so sure they knew everything about the arthouse cinema, even though it was she, not them, who was Jackson – the nice, soft, good-looking Access to Media lecturer's – favourite, partly because she was pretty but also because she was clever ...

She realised Jackson was watching her, but only from the corners of her very hazy eyes. She could tell that he wanted to touch her again and the achy, prickly anticipation of it brought a rush of blood to her cheeks. It had been so long since someone had loved her, physically, that she had forgotten what being loved could feel like, and yet she wanted, with a desperate, passionate, somewhat hazy ache, for someone nice and soft and good-looking to try and make her remember ...

'But you never answered my question Miss Kat-ar-zy-na?'

'Your question?'

'Do you want another drink?'

'What? Here?'

'Well yes, unless ... unless you want to go somewhere else?'

Kathy paused, and then closed her eyes and remembered and then forgot everything that she was supposed to remember simultaneously. She wasn't thinking of him or of Eoin or of anything that she could name, just the sensation of someone else's fingers running through her hair, and the way in which it had ached and prickled down her spine ... And then a clinking sound pulled her back into the remainder of the evening. She opened her eyes again and saw that one of the girls from behind the bar was collecting empty glasses, gripping each one by the stem, until she held a translucent bouquet.

Heartache

STAN WALKED DOWN THROUGH THE Meadows, past St Flannan's, which was deserted, and then past Margaret's house, where the curtains were still drawn; and then he thought, just as he always did when he walked through this part of town, of how much the architecture reminded him of Gdańsk, and in particular the meanly angled flat in which he'd spent his childhood, at first with his mother, father and older brother, but then only his mother, who, after his father and older brother were taken from them, just sat in the flat and cried . . .

Stan carried on walking, across the river and into West Bridgford, which he preferred on account of its Englishness, and because of the way in which the houses grew and spread out around him until there were gardens and garages, and endless mock Tudor façades, each of which was edged by privet hedges. Then after a while he stopped, and placed his fat, pink finger very firmly on one of the new old-fashioned buzzers. Almost immediately the door opened and a neat blonde woman, who looked a bit like Iwona but older, peered round it and said, 'Hello, you must be Stan. I'm Madeleine, David's mother.'

Stan shook Madeleine's hand and followed her into the hallway, taking in the pale Farrow & Ball coloured walls, the bare wooden floorboards and the seagrass rug; and then he thought, as he always did when he visited these types of houses, that it wasn't very warm, or cozy. Accordingly, he removed his jacket, exposing the 'I Beat Anorexia' tee-shirt that lurked beneath it, and Madeleine burst into tinkling laughter.

'I am what you call the joker, yes?' said Stan.

'Quite. Now let me show you what needs fixing.'

Stan followed her into the kitchen, which was a similarly bleak pale grey, and watched while she demonstrated what the problem with the drawer was.

'Now can I get you something to drink?' she said, and Stan thought, as he always did, when talking to these types of women in these types of houses, that it was no use asking for a beer.

'The tea would be very nice thank you yes,' he said instead, and then, 'and if it is possible with the lemon and not the milk.'

Madeleine laughed her tinkling laugh again.

'Sounds like you're quite the sophisticate!'

'No just Polish.'

He opened his toolbox and had just begun to rummage inside when Madeleine handed him a china mug. Out of politeness he stopped what he was doing, took a sip, and then with genuine surprise said, 'This is good tea, very good, yes. Full of esencja.'

'Eseni ...?'

'Esencja. It is like the essence of the teas so you speak.'

Madeleine tinkled one last time while simultaneously stepping back towards the hallway.

'Well I'll leave you to get on then.'

Stan took another sip of tea and put the mug down on the side. Then he removed the drawer from underneath the hob and unscrewed the broken runner. It was a straight-forward enough job, requiring little concentration. Consequently, he hummed to himself as he worked, as well as listened, to the low burr of an older man's voice drifting through from the room next door, and Madeleine's higher one sailing over the top of it: 'Yes well he seems like quite a character ...'

Stan stopped and took another sip of tea, and then pulled hard at the remaining fragment. It broke away in sharp, oily bits that smeared his palms with black. Not wanting to dirty his surroundings he took one of the newspapers out of the recycling bin, unfolded it and laid it out across the worktop. He rarely used the Internet, which he viewed as a confusing fad, and he rarely read texts in English besides those he needed for his work, or, occasionally, the sports pages of *The Sun*, meaning that any news that came via anything other than a Polish radio station usually took a week or more to reach him. Now, however, he found himself looking at a photograph of an English soldier, whose expression was one of sulky, almost pouty, insolence. He reminded Stan of Ian McShane, in his *Lovejoy* days, and his likeness to him was so arresting that the whole image appeared to throb with technicolour panic. Looking at it he spluttered: 'Panu Bogu *świeczkę*, a diabłu ogarek!'

Which literally translated as:

A candle for God, a stub for the devil!

Which actually translated as:

I knew it! I knew it! God help me!

But despite Stan's protestations the face that had kissed his Kasia, and most probably more besides, continued to stare back up at him. And then, very gradually, it merged with the broken bodies in the background and transformed itself into a snake. And then it began, very slowly, to wrap itself around his chest. And then it stayed there, holding him and crushing him for what seemed like hours but which, according to his watch, couldn't have been more than a minute or two at most – and then, just when he thought he was about to breathe his last, it left him.

Nevertheless, Stan continued to remain where he was, unthinking and unmoving. And then, only when he had caught his breath, and blinked his eyes, and wiped the sweat from his brow, was he able to resume even a little of his former ease, carefully folding up the paper, and then putting it back in the recycling bin so that, for the present moment at least, Eoin no longer existed.

And only then, when the world was reassuringly drab and safe and bleak, pale grey again, did he decide that, seeing as he had already done everything that he was meant to do he might as well finish up and go and get a beer.

Headache

MEG WATCHED HER REFLECTION IN the glass of the train window, lit by the carriage's harsh, electric light. She knew that as soon as she arrived her mother would start berating her for her lack of hair, which she would equate with her lack of a husband, which Meg would in turn equate with the absence of Dave and their relationship, which, or so she believed, was already beginning to unravel ...

Although Meg's extended family in India regarded their religion as something that happened in the background of their lives, her immediate family, in Leicester, kept it at the heart of their existence. Her parents' marriage, which had the added glamour of being preceded by a courtship which had taken place in foreign climes – i.e. Nottingham – had not been arranged. Rather it had developed over time as they attended numerous lectures and parties together, as well as canvassing for the Red Rose Socialist Club, and, under her mother's duress, the Leicestershire Black Sisters – a fact that both her parents now seemed, most conveniently, to have forgotten. Whenever Meg's single status was mentioned, which had begun to happen with increasing regularity, it was always in relation to the sons of friends who 'shared their values' (a trait which appeared to refer as much to solid, dependable lifestyles as their ethnicity or religion). Consequently, her reluctance to visit the temple was not, as Dave had implied, a rejection of her Indian heritage, but of the banality of her English present:

Meghana Budannavar almost exists between Nottingham and Leicester, but sometimes dreams of Bangalore, where her parents, the Budannavars Senior, hail from. In their youth, the Budannavars Senior aspired to be more British than the British but are now, as they near retirement, more Indian than the Indians. Unlike their children, or even their children's children, the Budannavars Senior's religion or belief is mainly Hindu (or, more specifically, Lingayat) but sometimes No Religion and sometimes Other (although they have never felt any obligation whatsoever to explain this, their last vague statement) . . .

And then she began again:

Meghana Budannavar almost exists between dreams of England and of India . . .

And again:

Meghana Budannavar almost exists between dreams . . .

And again:

Meghana Budannavar almost exists . . .

And then she grew bored.

The train drew into the station and ground to a halt. Meg put on her expensive new coat, and her buy-one-get-one-free red bobble-hat, picked up the same rucksack that she had had since she left the first of her homes, in Leicester, and wriggled into the straps. And as she clomped through the streets which, thanks to Diwali, then Christmas, plus the ongoing sales, never seemed to get dark, and towards her home that was Indian, and English, and a retro-English version of the former, her mind travelled also, until she was back in the temple with Dave – although this time she decided to avenge herself by redacting the memory until it contained only the holiest of thoughts, and sometimes even chanting ...

She took out her phone, saw that she had one new text message, and put it back again without reading what it said. It buzzed again, but this time she didn't even bother to look at it. Instead she thought about whether Dave had ever really fancied her, or just an idea of her, or just an idea. And then about whether or not he had fancied any of the other women in the Cross-Cultural Identities Research Group, who had come in all sorts of colours. And then about whether or not he had ever really fancied anyone in any more than a half-hearted absent-minded way because that was about all his half-hearted absent-minded brain could cope with. And whether this was because he was too busy being 'spiritual but not religious'. Or 'religious but not spiritual'. Or 'magikal [sic] but not religious'. Or 'magikal [sic] and religious'. Or 'magikal [sic] and no belief' ... And then she thought that, whatever he perceived his context as, and thus hers in relation to it, she would have to ask, and if necessary, challenge him, both with regard to this, his sexual predilections, and his magikal affiliations. Only in order to do so he would have to pay her some attention, and, at least temporarily, take a break from working on his stupid, sick-inducing blog. And then she thought that one night in Leicester was enough and that she would catch the first train back tomorrow ...

Eggs Louis IX: A Magikal Cleansing Recipe

EGGS LOUIS IX APPROPRIATES ELEMENTS of infomagik and voo-doo, and then repurposes them across both the physical and digital realms. By transferring the malevolent energy of The Media into the as yet unfertilised egg, the magician is able to release any form of hex that they or the person they are working on behalf of may have fallen victim to via The News on Paper and/or The News on Television and/or The News Online. The charged eggs can either be broken, and so destroyed immediately, or used as a component within other rites (although this would constitute an extremely strong and dangerous magik and should therefore only ever be attempted by the most highly experienced magicians).

INGREDIENTS:
3 large free-range eggs
A selection of broadsheet and tabloid newspapers
A television set tuned to the news
A computer connected to the Internet

STATEMENT OF OFFENCE:
Committing a civil offence contrary to Section 70 of the Army Act 1955, that is to say a war crime contrary to Section 51 of the International Criminal Court Act 2001, namely inhuman treatment of a person protected under the provisions of the Fourth Geneva Convention 1949 as

defined by article 8(2)(a)(ii) of Schedule 8 of the said International Criminal Court Act 2001 and the International Criminal Court Act 2001 (Elements of Crimes) Regulations 2001.

1. Take the first large free-range egg and roll it over the selection of broadsheet and tabloid newspapers saying 'extract date of the offence'.
2. Strongly visualise the words from the broadsheet and tabloid newspapers entering the egg and turning the yolk black.
3. Take the second large free-range egg and roll it over the television set tuned to the news, saying 'extract time of the offence'.
4. Strongly visualise the words from the television set tuned to the news entering the egg and turning the yolk green.
5. Take the third large free-range egg and roll it over the computer connected to the Internet, saying 'extract, if appropriate, citation of relevant provisions'.
6. Strongly visualise the words from the computer connected to the Internet entering the egg and turning the yolk red.
7. Say the Statement of Offence.
8. Either break the eggs into a bowl to release the malevolent energy, or store in a cool dry place.

Erzulie Balianne/
The Immaculate Heart

MEG WALKED UP PAST THE still, silver lake, the pale-pink ice cream kiosk and the glossy-green rhododendron bushes, and towards the geography department. As she rounded the corner she saw two boys sitting on a bench, both of them wearing the same Stop the War Coalition badges as her. They were holding giant paper cups of coffee as if they were miniature hot-water bottles, and, looking at them, Meg laughed and said, 'This isn't cold.'

The boys held her gaze for a second, and then stared at the ground in front of them, while Meg carried on her way. Then, as soon as she arrived at the entrance she went inside, and then wound her way along the warm bureaucratic corridors until she reached the room at the far end. Then she knocked, and listened for the familiar squeak of floorboards, except that this time there was only silence until, without warning, Professor Woźniak flung the door open.

'Ah Meg, good to see you. Come in, come in, sit down.'

Meg started slightly, and then, regaining her composure, followed him inside. Then she removed her expensive new coat, and her new buy-one-get-one-free blue beret, and took up her usual position in the chair opposite his desk.

'So Meg ...' said Professor Woźniak stroking his moustache.

'Yes?'

'So, err, yes ...'

186

'My thesis?'

'Err, yes, your thesis.'

Professor Woźniak took out a cigarette and lit it, an action that reminded Meg that different, in some ways more liberal, rules applied to the different, in some ways more liberal, world of the university, such as being allowed to smoke indoors, but also narrower ones, such as never being allowed to use the pronoun 'I', or to talk in terms of what you liked, let alone held dear . . .

'Well, I think that it's pretty much finished,' she said, after a moment or so. 'I mean I know that the final hand-in isn't for a few months but . . .'

'But you're happy?'

'With what I've written?'

'Yes, exactly.'

'Yes. Very.'

Professor Woźniak took a drag on his cigarette, and let his eyes rest upon Meg's lack of hair. Then he took another drag, stroked his moustache and said, 'I don't know if you're aware of it, but there's a research post coming up.'

'Yes, I'm aware of it.'

'Well then I would encourage you,' and on the word 'encourage' Professor Woźniak actually winked, 'to apply.'

Instinctively Meg put her hands up over her ears, which were most definitely not her best feature, and very slowly nodded. She knew that this was the nicest possible thing that he could have said to her, because by saying it he was also offering her the chance to pursue the career that, until now, she had always claimed she wanted; and yet she was shocked to discover that the thought of it, and of the neat practical life that would follow, actually made her whole body go limp with fear. She tried to concentrate on the piles of papers in front of her, removed her hands and said, 'Well the thing is, I might not be here next year.'

'Oh? Really? And where will you be?'

'Err . . . India perhaps.'

'You have family there?'

'Yes. But I want to go as a tourist. I want to discover who I am.'

'Or who you plan to be?'

'Yes. Exactly.'

Meg fingered the locket that hung, as always, around her neck and looked down at her shoes, which had scuffed toes. It was the first time that she had considered either India, or indeed any other alternative to her well-mapped-out career, but now that she had voiced it – this daring and poetic and romantic thing, this desire for freedom and for travel – she realised not only that she wanted it but also that she would do it.

'Well in that case . . .' Professor Woźniak handed her a piece of paper, 'some very minor revisions before the final hand-in.'

'Oh yes, thank you.'

'And then of course we'll have to have a talk about your viva.'

'Oh yes, yes we will.'

'And if you do happen to change your mind then drop me a line. These things don't come along very often you know.' Professor Woźniak let his eyes rest, for a second time, upon what remained of her hair, or maybe her ears. 'And Meg . . .'

'Yes?'

'Just . . . take care.'

Meg stood up and said goodbye, and then almost skipped out of the building, down past the rhododendron bushes that would soon burst into flame, and towards the beautiful, glittering lake and the rather quaint ice cream kiosk beside it. And all the while her mind raced with possibilities, like how many shifts at Waterstones it would take to buy a plane ticket to India, and how many to save enough to live for six months over there, which would definitely be cheaper than six months over here, where everything went on clothes that didn't suit her . . .

As she rounded the corner she almost collided with the same two boys that she had encountered earlier, but who were now standing up, shivering. They each held one side of a newspaper, the first two pages of which were covered in pictures of smiling English soldiers, and the ruined flesh of their prisoners lying in a pyramid beneath. The first boy pointed to it and said, 'I can't believe that this could happen.' And then threw his empty coffee cup on the ground.

Meg paused, and a second later picked it up. And then she scrunched the paper cup into a paper ball and threw it in the bin.

Agasou/St Louis IX, King of France

DAVE PUT DOWN THE CARDBOARD box and arranged himself on top of it. He reached inside his jacket in search of cigarettes, and then, as soon as he found them he lit up. Meg, however, continued briskly removing the rest of the boxes from the car until all of the various, useless items that he had only recently packed up and taken back to his parents' house in West Bridgford were stacked on the pavement outside his new bedsit in Forest Fields. Then she slammed the boot shut, turned towards him and said, 'I wish you hadn't started smoking again. It's like kissing an ashtray.'

'Ah Meg come on—'

'No you come on. Come on and help me get these boxes – I mean your boxes – inside.'

Dave stubbed out his almost untouched cigarette and put it back inside the packet. He knew that she was annoyed, partly because he had decided not to move into one of the flats that she had suggested, or suggested that they move in together, and partly because she was nervous about handing in her thesis – although whenever he'd tried to discuss this latter anxiety she'd denied it, and then used India to try and distract him.

Reluctantly, he picked up one of the boxes, and followed her into the building and up the first flight of stairs. As soon as he reached the top, the bottom of the box he was carrying gave way, spilling all of the books inside it out onto the landing. The door opposite him immediately opened, and a young woman in a long, embroidered cotton dress appeared and said, 'Is everything alright?'

'No,' said Meg.

'Yes, yes, sorry,' said Dave. 'We, I mean I, was just in the process of, err, of moving in and I, err . . .'

The young woman bent down and gathered up *The Kaosphere*, *Voodoo: A Beginner's Guide*, and one of the *Warhammer 40,000* novels. She turned it over carefully and said, 'So you're into fantasy?'

'Well, what I'm actually interested in is magik – with a "k" – but more specifically postmodern magik and—'

'But you've got a book on voodoo?'

'Well yes, voodoo is also an interest, but primarily in relation to syncretism as opposed to anything more, err . . . primitive.'

'I'm afraid I don't know what that means.'

'Primitive?'

'Syncretism.'

'It means combining different belief systems while blending the practices of different intellectual traditions,' said Meg, and then began to shove the remainder of the fallen books back inside the box. 'He's got a blog.'

'Oh really? I have a blog too. On crystal healing.'

Dave murmured something suitably polite but non-committal, picked up the box again and continued on his way. He expected Meg to do the same, only she stayed where she was, making unnecessary small talk, until, as he reached the top of the last flight of stairs and opened the door to what was now his bedsit, he heard her laugh and say: 'Oh don't mind him, he's just shy around new people,' as if he were a child, and then in a louder voice which he assumed was mainly for his benefit, 'but crystals are his passion. In fact, I'm sure that he'll want to have a good long chat with you about it. You really must pop round . . .'

Not wanting to hear anymore, he kicked the door shut. Then he took out the same cigarette he had been forced to abandon earlier and relit it. And then, when Meg finally re-joined him, he sat down and watched, without offering to help, as she opened

191

up one of the boxes, removing the curtains that his mother had bought for him from Habitat, followed by the cushions that Meg had bought for him from IKEA, one of which she now placed on the chair beneath the window.

'It's bad enough that you have to take the piss out of me all the time, but why do you have to involve that girl downstairs?' he said eventually.

'Ah Dave come on—'

'No you come on, come—' and then, realising that he was mimicking their earlier exchange, he stopped, stubbed out his first cigarette and lit a second.

Meg picked up another one of the cushions, sat down upon it and wriggled closer to him. She plucked the cigarette out of his hand and took a drag, and straight away her eyes began to fill with tears, although whether this was from the smoke or something else, Dave could not be sure. So he took another drag and waited, and after a moment Meg turned to him and said, 'Is this because I cut my hair?'

For the first time he was genuinely taken aback. 'No, no of course not,' he said, quickly, and in his agitation, he let a piece of ash fall onto and burn his hand. 'Don't be stupid, I mean, err, silly.'

'Then why did you change your mind about my parents' puja?'

'I already told you, I had to work on my blog.'

Meg put her hands up over her ears, and in response Dave shifted uncomfortably. He knew that the blog sounded like a poor excuse, even if it was a true one, but now that he had found his own religion it wasn't as if he needed hers, just as now that she herself had become a certainty in his life, or so he believed, it wasn't as if he had to circle round her second-guessing what she wanted. Dimly he wondered if being her boyfriend meant that he should buy her flowers, or make some other traditionally romantic gesture so as to alleviate his guilt, and yet he also feared that they were both too cynical either to give or to receive such gifts affectively ...

'Do you know what my name means?' Meg said at last, staring into the curtains.

'Err, pearl maybe? Or lily? I mean a lot of women's names tend to mean those things, or types of things and, err—'

'It means cloud.'

It was so unexpected that Dave laughed, and then, still laughing, he put his arm around her waist and pulled her towards him, so that she was half standing, half sitting on his lap.

'And do you know what that means?' he asked, holding her tight while she gave in and shook her head against his heart. 'It means that we live in the sky, together.'

Erzulie Freda/
Our Lady of Sorrows

KATHY CLICKED OUT OF THE Free Ads screen and onto the Hotmail screen. She could see that Judy was headed in her direction but as there was only one more week to go until she was officially redundant, she no longer tried to disguise the fact. Instead she continued to type in her username and her password and then, to her surprise, no new or unread emails, which meant no new or unread emails from trolls or journalists flashed onto the screen. She had assumed that, by the time the story reached the proper newspapers, their number and ferocity would have increased, but in truth by the time the story had escaped the Internet they'd got bored. She cracked her knuckles, so that they made a sound like three eggs breaking, and then she clicked 'compose':

Dear Jackson,
    I've attached a copy of my application. If you've time to look through it, it would be much appreciated.
    Love,
        Kathy (aka Katarzyna) X

She pressed send, and then, before she had had time to translate what her request either might or might not mean, an answer pinged straight back:

Dear Katar-zy-zy-zy-na!

Yes of course. I've been meaning to get in touch. Are you free this weekend?

Love

Jackson X

And then, without any space to think in:

Yes. Text me the deets X

Kathy looked up and saw Aaeesha Begum reaching for the box of Milka chocolates that Sam from Motors' girlfriend had bought for him for work, but as soon as she saw Kathy, or so it seemed to Kathy, she looked away; and as soon as she looked away, Kathy was seized by a desperate need to have a very normal, very mundane conversation with her that would prove that nothing had changed, even though if nothing had changed then she would have avoided having any form of conversation altogether.

Kathy jumped up and darted over to the chocolates, but by the time she reached them Aaeesha had already sat back down. She took a chocolate anyway and, as soon as she put it in her mouth, she felt the hunger, that she hadn't even realised had been gnawing at her body, leave it – and then she took another and another and so on, each one of which tasted even better than the last.

'You know there's something different about you today Kathy,' said Judy, coming up behind her. 'I can't quite put my finger on it but . . .'

But something buzzed inside Kathy's pocket:

Y don't I pick U up at 6 on Sat? J X

And without pausing:

Sounds good. C U then K X

Kathy put her phone back inside her pocket along with two more of the chocolates, smiled and said, 'I can't resist!'

'I know, they're very moreish aren't they?'

'Umm . . .'

Kathy took a final chocolate and went back to her computer, her fingers veering instinctively towards 'compose'. She knew that Eoin had already been court martialed, and had already served half of his twenty-eight days, which meant that she knew that in another two weeks he would be inescapably hers. Yet the pride, which, until now, she didn't even know that she possessed, had suddenly made her desperate to avoid him . . .

Kathy looked up and saw Aaeesha heading back over towards the chocolates. She stood up again and once more darted after her. As soon as she reached them, she grabbed another handful, smiled and said, 'I can't resist!'

'But last time someone bought chocolates in you and Meg threw them in the bin,' said Aaeesha.

'I know, but these ones, well, they're very moreish aren't they?'

'Moreish?'

And then, not knowing what else to do besides regret her choice of words, she stuffed a chocolate in her mouth. Aaeesha watched her while she chewed and swallowed and then said, 'Yes I see.'

'You see what?'

'That you can't resist.'

'Oh, err, right,' said Kathy, and she felt her face colouring, with heat and blood and shame.

Baron Samedi/
St Martin de Porres

MARGARET LEANT ON BLESSINGS' ARM for a moment, and then bent over and, rather clumsily, rubbed her knees.

'Are you alright Margaret? Maybe we should stop and have a cup of tea?'

'No, no I'm fine thank you Blessings. I just want to finish my shopping and go home.'

'But there's a Starbucks over there. We could—'

'I said that I'm fine thank you Blessings.' And then, as soon as Blessings bowed her head, Margaret felt mean. 'It's only that Eoin arrives next week. And I want everything to be just right.'

'I know, but how can you take care of him if you don't take care of yourself? Father Jonathan—'

'Now that looks like just what we want,' Margaret broke in, and then took a step towards the Waterstones opposite. 'Come on Blessings.'

'But you already have a new calendar.'

'Yes, but it's a little too ... fiery.'

Again Blessings bowed her head, and then a moment later held out her arm, and the two women crossed the road. Margaret did not normally venture into bookshops, having had little time, since leaving school, for reading anything besides the Bible or *The Post*, and consequently the other shoppers, with their tote bags and baggy blazers, were not the kind that she was used to. She teetered, uncertainly, towards a table covered in notebooks, one of which had a picture of the Eiffel Tower on the cover, and underneath it the words 'La Tour Eiffel' embossed in gold.

'I'm afraid I don't know what that means,' said Margaret, tracing the letters with her finger. 'But it certainly looks very French. And it's only three pounds. Do you think that I should get it for Albertina?'

'I am sure that she would be very pleased,' said Blessings, and Margaret nodded, picked up the notebook and then clutched it, very tightly, against her chest.

'Now let me see, the calendars . . .'

Yet all of the calendars were arranged on the top shelves, too high up for her, or even Blessings to reach. Margaret craned her neck and looked helplessly from side to side until a young, brown-skinned woman appeared and said, 'Hello, can I help you?'

'Oh yes thank you, err . . .' Margaret's left eye moved down towards her name badge, while the right one flickered, 'Meg. I'd like "A Dog for All Seasons", but I think that you'll probably need to get a man to reach it.'

'Oh, it's no bother,' said Meg.

'Or just someone taller.'

'I really don't mind.'

'Or someone less . . .'

'Less . . .?'

Margaret watched as Meg clambered up onto one of the kick stools, pulled out a copy of 'Antique Maps 2005' and handed it to her.

'You've made a mistake,' she said, very sharply. 'I asked for "A Dog for All Seasons".'

'Oh I am sorry.' Meg replaced 'Antique Maps 2005', took down 'A Dog for All Seasons 2005', and handed it to her. 'Here you go.'

Margaret watched as she jumped down off the kick stool and flicked her hair out of her eyes. Then, as soon as she had walked off out of sight, she turned to Blessings and hissed, 'There's a reason that people don't like Muslims.'

Blessings looked shocked, and then from side to side to see if anyone else was listening. She smoothed her blouse and then, very calmly, said, 'The first president that we elected in Malawi was a Muslim. And he was very popular. We thought that—'

'You thought that there were no prospects.'

'Yes, no, there aren't but—'

'But God remembers the faithful,' said Margaret, once more feeling mean and now also desperate, and then, wishing to compensate for both these things, she reached out her hand – only instead of taking it Blessings started laughing.

'In the next life, yes, but not in this one.' And she continued to shake until the tears ran down her cheeks. 'In this one we're all lost.'

'But Blessings!'

'But it is true Margaret, very true. If Malawi was rich, then nobody there would pray.'

Margaret stared hard at her for a moment, and then, when Blessings still continued to shake as if seized by the spirit, or the devil – these days she really couldn't be sure – she took out her hearing aid and put it in her pocket. Then she unfolded her shopping list and stared at it instead, before striking a line through 'calendar – flowers or animals' and 'thank you present for Albertina'. And then she drew a circle around 'pyjamas' because the pair under what was still Eoin's pillow had worn right through and she mustn't forget to replace them.

Ogou Balanjo/St Joseph

STAN EXAMINED THE EXERCISE BOOK, which was opened in the centre of the kitchen table. Each page consisted of a list of Polish words scribbled in blue biro and a truncated English translation pencilled in beside them. There was also a pile of envelopes, all of which were full of receipts, and another, closed exercise book labeled 'cash only' – which meant that not all of the information inside necessarily needed to be declared, unlike the other book that one way or another was a definite proof of something.

Stan sighed, because he was already tired, and then sat down in front of the laptop that his daughter had lent him, and its screen that read, 'Sign in and file your Self Assessment Tax Return'. Then he logged onto his account, and began to enter the figures based on the open book into one of the virtual boxes, and then the figures based on the receipts inside the envelopes into another, and then he saw that, provided the shut book stayed shut, all was as it should be. He clicked 'submit', and the screen in front of him morphed into another screen that read, 'Thank you. Your Tax Return has been successfully submitted.'

Stan sighed again, but this time with relief. He went over to the fridge and took out a beer. As he uncapped the bottle he thought of his daughter, whom he loved, and Eoin O'Shea, whom he did not, and he felt the pain from last week returning. Then he put down the bottle, went back over to the laptop and typed 'www.

google.com' into the navigation bar, and then 'Eoin O'Shea' into the box beneath it, and line after line of video links appeared. He clicked on the first strip of characters and a succession of pop-up windows for online gambling, pornography and such like began to open out across the screen.

Stan clicked 'close' on the first of the pop-up windows, but almost immediately a dozen others sprang up in its place. He kept on clicking and clicking but the Internet was too fast for him. Not knowing what else to do, he held his fat, pink finger on the power button until the machine shut down. Then, at the exact moment that the screen went black, Iwona entered the kitchen.

'You're looking very shifty,' she said, in Polish.

'Am I?'

'Yes.' She put down the carrier bags she was carrying and moved closer to the table. 'What have you have been up to?'

'Oh nothing really, but I think that I accidently downloaded some sort of virus—'

'A virus? What on earth were you looking at?'

'Just the Self Assessment website, and then, well, I guess that I sort of googled Eoin—'

'Oh for goodness sake Stańko! First you decide to spy on Kasia and then while you're doing it you break her things.'

Iwona turned away from him and back towards the carrier bags. Her shoulders were raised in such a way that, even though it made only a very slight, almost imperceptible difference to her posture, Stan could tell she was annoyed. He watched as she firmly and precisely placed each item down upon the worktop, and opened a box of eggs, wriggling each one of them around inside the cardboard cups to check that they hadn't broken. He waited until she had finished and then, in what he hoped was a conciliatory voice, said, 'Look, next time I see Kasia I'll explain—'

'Well then you can explain tomorrow. She's coming here for her tea – although I won't be cooking anything fancy.'

'Right, well I'll . . .'

But instead of finishing his sentence he drained the rest of his beer, and then opened the fridge and got another, while doing his best to ignore the tone of Iwona's shoulders. Again he waited, this time while she filled the kettle, found a teabag and sliced a lemon; and then he continued to wait until she had sat down beside him, mug in hand. Then he tried again: 'I was concerned, that's all. You must have seen the papers.'

'And since when have you believed the papers?' said Iwona, in a voice that had most definitely seen the papers, and yet refused to see what was in them.

'But that's exactly why I looked.' He took another sip of beer and said, 'She's my daughter—'

'Our daughter.'

'Our daughter and . . .'

And then, without any warning, the pain was back, only this time it came with memories attached to it. The ones where he'd learned that his brother and then his father had died, for instance. Or the ones where he'd seen his father and then just his mother crying for them. Or the ones where Iwona had first come to England, and there had then been that terrible, indefinite period of uncertainty, where he'd woken up each morning thinking that he had lost her . . . On and on the memories kept on coming, until, having no other way of saying anything that should be said, he banged his fist upon the table.

'But what if it is true Iwona?' He finally spluttered as the grief moved downwards, and a new feeling, this time of nausea, welled up inside his stomach. 'What if it is and she marries him? What sort of life is that? For us? For them? For anybody? Tell me – what sort of life is that?'

Paddy

PADDY WAITED, NOT ONLY UNTIL the bus had pulled into the bus station and the driver had turned the engine off, but also until all of the other passengers had collected their belongings. He continued to wait as, one by one, they filed past him, stumbled down the stairs, and retrieved their larger luggage from the hold; as they all said 'thank you driver' to the driver, and the driver said 'cheers duck' back, and then went round with a carrier bag picking up their empty sandwich wrappers; and only then, when the bus was completely empty of excuses, did he begin, very slowly, to make his way along the aisle.

Paddy could see, through the gaps in the concrete pillars, that the sky outside was a washed-out English grey. There were a few girls with pushchairs in front of the poundshop, and an older lady pushing a tartan trolley. Although he knew that his Nana would probably have a new calendar by now, it occurred to him that it might still be a good idea to go and look for a present. He had missed Christmas after all, and didn't want to just turn up empty-handed . . .

Paddy slung his kitbag over his shoulder with what would have been determination, had determination not long since been replaced by continuing to function, just, and set off towards the city centre. Out of habit he walked with brisk, even steps. But inside his heart was racing, stopping and starting like machine-gun fire . . .

Paddy carried on walking until he reached the Body Shop. The window was filled with cardboard boxes, each of which contained a variety of creams on beds of shredded tissue. 'Smellies' – that's what women called them, a word that seemed as strange and alien as women themselves now did. 'Snakes with tits' – that's what one of his old army buddies had called women, after his wife had informed him, via text message, that she was leaving him for someone else . . .

'After anything in particular?'

Paddy looked through the shopgirl, and picked out one of the bottles on the shelf behind her. He held it up to his nose, and inhaled the scent of a sick peach. Then he turned it round so that he could see the label, which said 'Dewberry'. Despite the fact that, in recent months, he'd learnt numerous picturesque names for plants, on account of having seen numerous picturesque plants and, having little else to offer his fellow soldiers by way of conversation, had then always enquired as to the names of them, he couldn't help wondering if the dewberry, much like the clustered bellflower or blooming nightshade of Northern Iraq, might also be an hallucination, or some other type of thing that he'd unwittingly invented.

'Is it real?'

'I'm sorry?' said the shopgirl.

'Is it real? The dewberry?'

She looked confused, and then, as if suddenly deciding to take it as a joke, she laughed. Paddy was still wearing his army boots, but with jeans, and a well-ironed shirt tucked into them, and he knew that the figure he cut was a crisp and good-looking one, just as he knew too that this was the reason she had opted to turn her bewilderment into amusement, and not contempt . . .

'I think it must be,' said the shopgirl, 'or they wouldn't be able to make it into a body spray, would they?' She started to toss her hair, but then stopped, so that it fell into her face and not across her shoulders, 'Unless it's not a dewberry, but dew from a berry. I mean, in that case it could be any berry couldn't it? It could be a—'

'Gooseberry?'

She laughed again, resumed tossing her hair and said, 'Like it?'

'Err, it's okay.'

'For your girlfriend...?'

'No. My Nana.'

The shopgirl's face brightened. She led Paddy to a table covered in pink soap, and matching bath salts. This time they smelled of rose-scented drawer liners, which was apt, considering that it was the sort of thing his Nana would have immediately put in a drawer under the category 'for best'. Only the best is always yet to come, thought Paddy, with no emotion whatsoever, the best never comes and all that's been saved up for it festers ... He poked one of the soaps and said, 'I'll have a think about it.'

'Oh.' The shopgirl's face fell, and she quickly tried to pretend it hadn't. 'Well I'm always here if you need any advice, or ...?'

'I'll remember that, thanks.'

Paddy left the Body Shop and walked on, back around, and then down towards the Broadmarsh Shopping Centre, except that this time he took a different route that went past Marks & Spencer. Through the window he could see several middle-aged women loitering by the cardigans. Beside them was a stack of decorative tins containing biscuits. He knew this was one of the few gifts that Margaret would allow herself to enjoy, as the tin could be saved and then used to disguise a less expensive brand, meaning that the contents could be devoured guilt-free. Accordingly he entered, picked up the largest one that he could find, and turned towards the checkout – yet something held him back.

Without any warning, the something, which was almost a tear, but was actually an involuntary reflex action, began to form in the corner of Paddy's eye. He knew that his reluctance to make the purchase was odd, especially since, once he had done so he would be able to go home, and indeed, could be home, in under half an hour. He was tired, and if he went home he could sleep. He could go into what was still his bedroom, and draw the curtains that were still his curtains, and pull the duvet right up over his head, and stay there. Alone. In the dark ... But instead he put down the tin, picked up his kitbag, and carried on walking.

Fame and Glory

STAN SAT AT THE KITCHEN table and watched as his wife prepared their evening meal. True to her word, which in this particular case was indistinguishable from her irritation, Iwona had refused to cook 'anything fancy', which also meant anything Polish, which also meant anything heavy and fatty and filling, which was exactly the type of food he liked best. He watched as she rinsed and then sliced the tomatoes for their salad, and then stopped abruptly, with the knife raised in her hand.

'Kasia?' she said, in Polish and English, and then listened to the dull click and twist of their own front door. 'Kasia is that you?' And then, as soon as Katarzyna appeared, she let her arm drop back down against her side. 'You look different. I can't quite put my finger on it but ...'

Katarzyna smiled, opened the cutlery drawer and took out what they needed. She laid the table, and then as soon as she had finished she began to pick out the pieces of tomato from the salad, only stopping when Iwona slapped her wrist. His wife was right, Stan thought fondly, his daughter did look different, and not only that, she looked beautiful.

'You look beautiful,' he said.

Katarzyna laughed and reached for another piece of tomato, only this time Iwona moved what was left of the salad out of her way before she had chance to take it. She pointed at the cardboard box beside her and said, 'If you actually want to help me, then you could whisk those eggs together.'

Katarzyna nodded, removed a large glass bowl from one of the cupboards, opened up the cardboard box and took out an egg. She broke it onto the side of the bowl, and a pool of blood and slime immediately glopped out onto the bottom.

'Eww! Yuck! Gross!' she said, prodding at something that resembled a piece of gristle. 'What the fuck is that?!'

'Kasia! There is no need to swear,' said Iwona, and then, examining the bowl she added, 'It's the beginnings of a chick that's all. We must have got a fertilised one by mistake.'

Iwona scooped out what could have been the chicken or the egg and washed it down the sink. She cracked the remaining eggs into the bowl and whisked them all, very briskly together, and then poured the mixture into the frying pan, which was already warming on the stove.

'There, that's better. And now your father has something to tell you,' she said, her shoulders rising as she twisted the pan. 'Don't you Stańko?'

'Oh, oh yes,' Stan began, a little hesitantly. 'Well, yesterday I started doing my tax return – you're right it's much easier online – and then I was, you know, having a look on the Internet, and I think that at some point I may have downloaded a virus—'

'A virus? But what were you looking at?'

'Yes exactly,' said Iwona, and once more the lightning flashed across her shoulder blades. 'Please enlighten us.'

Stan paused, and as he did so he thought about how, even though after twenty-five years of marriage, he could sense his wife's irritation within a mere fraction of a second, it still took him many hours, or even days, to figure out the cause. Iwona, he now realised, was not insisting that he reveal his suspicions because she wanted to expose him, but because she too wanted to know whether or not his suspicions had any basis in reality ...

'Just the Self Assessment website,' he continued, but a little more confidently than before, 'and then I mean, I guess that I sort of googled Eoin—'

'But why were you googling Eoin?' said Katarzyna.

'Go on,' said Iwona, bending over the pan. 'Why were you?'

'Because . . .' And Stan turned from his wife's frightened shoulders to his daughter's frightened face, and braced himself because this was what it took, he felt, to be a husband, a father and some sort of decent man. 'Because of what I read in the papers. I wanted to know if-if . . . if it was true.'

There was silence, for he couldn't be sure how long and then: 'You don't have to worry. We broke up,' said Katarzyna.

'You broke up?' said Stan, unsure whether this was the truth or simply a ruse to get him and Iwona off her back.

'For good?' said Iwona, who must have also been wondering if and when Katarzyna and Eoin had actually spoken.

'Yes, for good,' said his beautiful daughter, before getting up and leaving the room.

Stan breathed out, and then opened the fridge and took out a bottle, which he placed against the table's edge. He hit the top of it, squarely, with his fist so that the cap popped off and a little beer spurted out onto the floor. He sighed again, with relief more than pleasure, and then he took a swig, and then another, and then another until the bottle was empty. Finally, Iwona moved away from the stove and sat down beside him, and then, very gently, he placed his arm around her shoulders.

Cloud

MEG CONTINUED TO REMOVE PIECES of her clothing, one by one, from the overstuffed rail. Occasionally she would take whatever she had just selected over to the mirror, and hold it up in front of her, turning this way and that, before then either returning it to its original place or, more often than not, throwing it, along with all of the others onto the pile beside the bed.

'But are you sure you want to get rid of quite so much?' said Kathy, picking up a pair of trousers.

'I can't take everything with me.'

'Couldn't you leave some things here? What about Dave? Or your parents?'

What about Dave, thought Meg, or my parents – neither of whom wanted her to go to India but all of whom wanted her to be an Indian in a million other ways – and then last but not least what about me? Me – who is religious *and* spiritual, but not religious and cultural. Nor spiritual and cultural. Nor anything else. Me – who has nonetheless found the courage to do something more daring and poetic and romantic than she ever thought possible? Me – thought Meg, again and again, throwing pieces of her clothing onto the floor. What about me and what I want, to be, or to become, right in this moment, now?

'And what about your viva?' said Kathy, picking up a dress and wriggling into it. 'You can't go away before that, surely?'

Meg paused and looked up, not at the rail, but at the books filled with case studies, and the files filled with photocopies of them, all of which were still arranged, alphabetically, across the walls, and wished that she could throw them on the pile as well; and then set fire to it, in a religiously and spiritually, but not culturally, Indian way until the present was gone, and she had no alternative but the future ... But instead she said, 'But I can Skype. And I've already saved enough to buy my ticket.'

'But why go *now*?'

'Because I don't want to wait for *then*.'

Meg made her way over to the mirror and held a blouse in front of her chest. Next to her own reflection she could also see Kathy's. Her mother, in one of her more pious and senior moments, had told her that the hair you were born with was the hair from your past life, and that this was the reason that Hindu (or, in her case, Lingayat) babies were shaved; and the thought that her own lost locks might be framed in this way, not as a source of regret, but as a symbol of rebirth, was one she found pleasing. She removed the blouse from the hanger, threw it onto the pile and said, 'That dress looks better on you, you should keep it.'

'Thanks,' said Kathy, who blushed and added, 'but how long will you be gone for?'

'I don't know. Definitely six months. Indefinitely? Who knows.'

'But won't Dave miss you?'

'He has a blog now.'

'But do you think that's enough?'

But do I think that's enough? thought Meg, as Kathy replaced her in front of the mirror, turning this way and that so that the dress fluttered out around her thighs. Yes, unfortunately, I do. She looked at Kathy's body, which said sex, whereas everything about her own body said denial; and yet at the same time it now seemed as though it was her body and her style that Kathy wanted ...

'You know you really should try wearing your hair up,' said Meg, examining Kathy's reflection through her own.

'Like this?' And Kathy piled her hair, loosely on top of her head.

'No, this.'

Meg stepped forward and scraped back all the strands in the same way that she used to scrape back hers every time she was annoyed and wanted, temporarily, to be sexless, and Kathy's eyes and cheeks became a series of stark flat stripes. It made her look older but also more elegant, and again more like Meg, or what Meg used to be, before she had moved, religiously and spiritually, beyond it.

Something Fine or Fortunate

MARGARET ARRANGED THE CUPS, QUICKLY and clumsily, upon the tray and then did the same with the biscuits which, even though it was the most special of special occasions, were still shop-bought, because even the thought of creaming the sugar and butter together was enough to make her clawing hands and her crumbling knees ache until there was no room for anything besides it. Then, as soon as the water had boiled, she picked up the kettle and filled up the teapot, chipping the spout in her haste.

'Now you'll have a cup of tea won't you Eoin? And there's biscuits too if you'd like.'

'Aye Nana a cup of tea would be grand.'

Margaret shuffled back into the front room, set everything down, and then straight away began to pour, only an uneven stream of water immediately splashed across her blouse, turning the lilac to indigo. Eoin took the teapot from her and said, 'Here Nana, let me.'

'But you're—'

'I said let me.'

Margaret pressed her lips together and perched on the edge of an armchair while Eoin poured out a cup. She thought that he had such nice hands. And that they were a bit like Steven's hands. And that he had such a nice way about him, and always had. That he knew how to be gentle without being effeminate, and to take care

213

of you without making you feel grateful. And that deep down he was still the same anxious, lovable, heartbreaking little boy who had come to live with her all those years ago ... And then she let him help her grip her cup, while she looked down at the spots on her blouse – which resembled the tears of a saint – and then up at the mantelpiece opposite, where a litter of puppies tumbled across the top half of the calendar, and the bottom stated that it was July 2005.

'I think you're getting a bit ahead of yourself there Nana,' said Eoin, and nodding at the mantelpiece added, 'it's only the second of Feb.'

'I know, I know, but February was a very snooty poodle, and then I remembered how much you wanted a puppy.'

The low rumbling sound of Eoin's laughter travelled around the room. Margaret looked at him uncertainly, and as she did so her eyes began to prick with holy water; because although she could see that her grandson looked alright on the outside, which looked exactly the same as before, and although she knew that he was still anxious, and lovable and heartbreaking and was indeed breaking her own, already damaged heart right now, she knew too that there was something else there on the inside, where the army and the Muslims had hurt him ...

'I know that you must miss your dog,' she said carefully, and then, 'was there no way that you could have brought him with you?'

'I don't think so Nana, it's only soldiers that get discharged I'm afraid, not animals.'

'But what if he bit someone he shouldn't have?'

'Well then I suppose they'd have to put him down.'

The words 'bring back hanging' and then 'hanging's too good for them' flashed through Margaret's mind. That's what all the papers had said about the IRA during the Troubles, and that's what all the Irish had thought about the Orangemen from time immemorial, and that's what she thought, when she thought about herself, and her own failures towards her family now.

She pressed her lips together again and contemplated the statuette of Our Lady that was now stood, serenely, between

214

two of the puppies, whose giant red mouths and giant amber eyes slobbered and glinted above her. Then she tried, and just about succeeded, in taking a bite of her biscuit, looked back at her grandson and said, 'You really must eat something Eoin. When I was in hospital people kept on telling me how much I needed sugar.'

'Sugar? That doesn't sound very healthy.'

'Well it is. It stops you from fainting.'

Eoin gave an awkward smile, and then picked up one of the biscuits and ate it very quickly. As soon as he had finished, Margaret said, 'You know I could do you an egg on toast if you're hungry.'

'But Nana I'm fine, and you're the one who has been ill. So it really should be me who is helping you.'

'But ...'

But Eoin had already begun to stack their cups together, along with what was left of the biscuits on the tray. Then he stood up and disappeared into the kitchen while Margaret put in her hearing aid and turned the volume up as high as it would go. She could hear what she took to be the sound of Eoin filling the sink with water, and then silence, which she took to be the sound of Eoin thinking, possibly about her, or Kathy, or even his mother in the same way that she too thought of his mother, her daughter, and sometimes her husband Steven; and then she looked back at Our Lady of Everything, the colour of whom matched her tears.

Do thou, bright Queen, O star of the sea,
Pray for thy children, pray for me.

'Sorry Nana what was that?' said Eoin, returning from the kitchen.

'Hail Queen of Heaven,' said Margaret, and then passed her hand across her face to hide her flickering eyelids. 'You've heard me sing it before, it's just that I don't always reach the end.'

Of Flowers

KATHY STOOD IN THE CENTRE of the room wearing a dress that had once been Meg's. Everything was cold and white except the dress, which was a festive poinsettia red, so that whenever she caught a glimpse of her reflection in the window she thought of a fire in the arctic, or a fire in an igloo, or any other type of fire that would eventually die out.

Kathy stood in the centre of the cold, white room in Forest Fields, which she had turned cold and white by painting it a colour that at the time had seemed clean and modern. It occurred to her that no one but her had been inside the room since Eoin had last been there. And then she began to worry that the sheets on the bed needed changing, and that the towels in the bathroom needed washing, and then that the whole place had a shut-up fusty smell that she couldn't smell anymore because she'd gotten so used to it.

Kathy stood in the centre of the cold, white room wearing what had once been Meg's expensive dress and worrying about non-existent smells, and then the world around her shattered. A small stone lay on the floor in front of the window, and there were shards of glass around it. She remained where she was for a moment, trying to work out what had happened, and then she began to edge, very slowly, along one of the walls until she reached the window. Very cautiously she looked out through the hole that was now in the middle of it.

'Kathy? Kathy is that you?' shouted Jackson.

'What are you doing?' Kathy shouted back.

'Just letting you know I'm here.'

'But there's a doorbell.'

'I was trying to be romantic. I didn't realise that it would actually break the glass.'

Kathy went to the door and pressed the buzzer that released the lock on the entrance to the block of flats, and then went back to the hole in the window and watched Jackson as he disappeared. She listened to his tread on the stairs, which was both lighter and more definite than Eoin's, and then the click of the front door opening and closing, and then Jackson was standing in the cold, white room beside her.

'Oh shit, I'm really sorry,' he said, looking down at the glass on the floor.

'Don't worry my dad can fix it.'

'But you'll freeze to death in the meantime.'

Kathy smiled a nice good smile, because it would have been impossible to explain that it would have been impossible for the cold, white room to get any colder, and then when it became weird to keep on smiling, she went into the kitchen, found an old cardboard box, a Stanley knife and a roll of parcel tape and brought them all back into the front room with her.

'Here, you can patch it up with this.'

'Okay . . .' said Jackson, looking up at the hole in the window, and then down at the cardboard box.

'I don't mind helping.'

'No, no, I insist.'

Kathy stood back and watched as Jackson began to cut through the cardboard, not by making one shallow groove and going back over it so that the piece you wanted came away in a crisp clean line, but by hacking randomly at it in a way that made the wrong-sized edges ragged. Then, when he had finished, he placed it against the pane, and then had to use almost all of the parcel tape to try to cover it.

217

'Oh shit, I'm really sorry,' he said again, stepping back from the window, 'DIY isn't really my forte.'

'Don't worry, my dad can fix it,' Kathy said again.

'Yeah but that won't exactly make a good impression on your dad.'

'And do you want to make a good impression on my dad?'

'Well I'd rather not make a bad one.'

Kathy was about to laugh, but then stopped and watched what could have been a blush creeping up Jackson's neck. She found the idea that he, the Access to Media lecturer, might now be embarrassed by his inability to mend a broken window surprising; and then she found that with this surprise came a kind of tenderness that lessened the gap between them.

'So where are we going for our tea then?' said Kathy.

'Luigi's. Do you know it?'

'I don't know anything about food.'

'I don't either really. Except Italian, but only because of my gap year. Sei la ragazza più bella che abbia mai visto.'

Kathy looked at Jackson and felt her own face turn to milk and blood and flowers. All the tenderness that had been there, just a few seconds ago, was now twisting itself into fear of those who knew more and those who knew better. She forgot that Jackson could only speak a few lines of one other, non-English language, whereas she was bilingual, and remembered only that she would one day have to run away from him in much the same way that she had had to run away from English Martyrs.

'I don't understand what you just said,' she said, and then touched the side of her face, which felt hot.

'It just means that you look nice,' said Jackson, and then touched her cheek with his own cold fingers. 'Although also kind of different. You should wear your hair like that more often.'

'But I'm worried that it makes me look older,' she said, turning this way and that, as though watching herself in an imaginary mirror.

'But you are older,' said Jackson, and then he laughed and tried to kiss her. 'It's what education does to you.'

Beloved

DAVE SHOOK HIS EMPTY CIGARETTE packet, patted his empty wallet and wondered if he should give up smoking again. He had only been in his bedsit a few weeks, and already his blog had lots of entries, which were getting lots of hits, and yet the gratification that he gleaned from both these things was somehow less than he had been expecting.

Dave looked at the Habitat curtains that his mother had bought for him, and then at the IKEA cushions that Meg had bought for him. He shook the cigarette packet one last time and threw it into the empty corner beside the bed for which neither Meg nor his mother had yet bought a bin, and then slapped his palm, hard, against his forehead.

Then he jumped up, switched on his laptop, and in an increasingly agitated manner began to type, until the words 'Post-Modern Magik: A User's Manual' sparkled across the screen. It had taken days to write the code necessary to achieve this effect, where the colours in each letter moved like diamonds or stars or carefully programmed pixels even, but as he continued, repeatedly, to tell himself, the result was very much worth it. He clicked on the words 'log in' in the top right-hand corner of the page, and then entered his email and password and clicked on 'update blog', and a new feeling began to come over him, that if he didn't do *something important immediately* then everyone, everywhere, would forget that he existed.

Dave jumped up again and began to pace around his bedsit, which meant taking four strides one way, and two strides the other. After a few minutes of this his eye lighted on a bag filled with hair, which he then picked up and repositioned next to his laptop. Then he went into the kitchen and opened the fridge, which contained only a box of eggs two weeks past their best before date. He removed one of the eggs, took it back to his laptop, and once again sat down, only this time he stared not at the screen but at the picture of Meg pinned to the wall behind it.

The background consisted of garland upon garland of marigolds, strung one on top of the other until the whole of the tiny rectangle seemed to be heaving and swaying in the dappled orange light, while Meg stood in the foreground, dressed in a bright-blue sari. The edges of the fabric were trimmed with gold, and there was also gold in her ears, her nose, on her neck and on her fingers, as well as in what had once been her hair, but which was now in a bag beside him ...

Dave continued to look at the photograph, which had been taken in Bangalore, a place to which Meg would soon be returning, and a place to which he had never been or indeed been asked to go. He knew that it was less the thought of their being apart that concerned him as the idea that she could quite easily do without his being there. Although he had tried to ignore her lack of interest in his blog, and in what he regarded as his recent, admittedly somewhat unconventional, career advancements, it was beginning to eat away at him – surely if he, as her future part-time house husband, were able to support her in all that she did, then she, as his current, full-time neurosis, could at least try to believe in him a little?

Dave continued to look at the photograph of the woman he had loved, without hope, for the last three years, but who, for the last three months, had appeared to share his feelings. He was aware of the numerous ways she had reignited his faith in his own destiny, but also how impermanent this faith was. How it waxed and waned in direct accordance with what he perceived as her desire for him, and how her encroaching absence was symbolic of the absence in his own life of any reasonable plan, or passion . . .

Dave shut his eyes, and then reopened them. And then he picked up one of the rotten eggs and threw it, so that it smashed against the blue and marigold part of the wall. The yolk slithered fatly over Meg's face, her jewellery, her sari, what had once been her hair until the whole of the image was a uniform orange, through which she stared, passive-aggressively, back at him.

14.02.2005

I did start to write. I just never finished. Or pressed send. Perhaps if I'd done better at school I'd have found the words, and known how to use them, correctly, or even meaningfully. I'd have known how to explain. But then again, if I'd done better I probably wouldn't need to . . .

EOIN O'SHEA CLOSED THE DIARY. It was small enough to slip into a shirt pocket, and came with a miniature pencil that slotted in the spine. Inside, each double-page spread was divided into eight boxes, one for every weekday, with just enough space for a few lines of writing underneath it, and one with an 'inspiring' quote, which in this particular instance was: 'Remember, if plan A didn't work there's still 25 more letters!' He looked across at the sunset, which was turning the dilapidated yellow brick buildings along the side of the road into a mouthful of broken and rotten teeth. It was the same as every other view, he thought dolefully, and the only difference was that sometimes you noticed it, and sometimes you didn't.

Eoin drew the curtains. He was twenty-six years old. A man and then some. And yet the decor of his room did not reflect this. The wallpaper, curtains and carpet, which had been chosen by his Nana, were decorated with large floral patterns, which clashed badly with the black ash furniture he'd chosen when he was fourteen. Other than this it was empty of belongings besides a large, outdated computer, a birthday card with a footballer on the front, and a brown paper bag from the Body Shop.

The Body Shop bag was a recent addition. Yesterday he had gone back there, and bought a bottle of perfume. Not the sick peach that he had tried last time, or one from the old-fashioned-drawer-liners-range, but another type called White Musk, which smelled of hairspray and fresh washing, both of which he associated, to some extent, with Kathy. He had bought it intending to go round to her flat afterwards, and had pictured the scene that would follow, where she fell, like blossom, into his arms – only, for some reason he couldn't quite articulate, he had asked the shopgirl out instead.

Eoin knew that one of the reasons why he couldn't quite articulate his reasons was because, although he could see why a lot of other men would think that the shopgirl was attractive, she wasn't the type of person he was usually attracted to. And the way she had tried to flirt, by which he meant the way she had simpered at him, was similarly unappealing. Kathy, on the other hand, was the most beautiful woman he had seen in his life, although she had never seemed to be more than fleetingly aware of it, or desperate for it, despite being so good at it. And Kathy was someone he loved . . .

Eoin opened the Body Shop bag, took out the perfume and sprayed it on his wrist. Then he held his wrist against his nose and closed his eyes. He listened, and tried not to listen, to the sounds of his Nana shuffling downstairs, and, for that moment, it was almost as if Kathy was there with him. Then he opened his eyes and sprayed the perfume all over his tee-shirt. And then he lay down on the single divan bed that he had had since he was ten years old and had first come to live here, by himself, with his Nana, pulled the tee-shirt up so that it covered the entirety of his face, and breathed in, very slowly.

Eoin breathed in and then breathed out again, letting his chest rise and fall in a steady, soothing rhythm. It was something he did often now, a means to prevent the last six months from crawling in and stopping him from being alone. That was not to say that he

223

liked being alone (he didn't), only that he liked being with other people even less. It was another of the things, along with avoiding Kathy and trying to date the shopgirl, that he couldn't quite articulate the reasons for; and as if to illustrate the ridiculous nature of his own, specific and personal hopelessness, his mobile beeped:

Hey Ian, hope we're still on for tonight. Looking forward to a very BERRY time! X

Eoin pulled his tee-shirt back down and sat up on the bed. He looked at the text message and then at the bottle of White Musk. Then he got up, turned the computer on, and logged onto his email – but nothing, bar one from one of his old army buddies who, like all of his old army buddies, he did not want to see, or hear from, ever again. Without opening it he pressed 'delete', and then 'refresh', and then 'refresh', and then 'refresh' – but nothing. Because after weeks and then months of being ignored, Kathy had finally gone away ... He sighed, turned off the computer, and picked up his phone:

Sure, where do you want to meet?

And almost immediately a reply pinged back:

Cucamaras? X

Eoin considered the text message, which was now not only an invitation to meet, and possibly sleep with, a girl to whom he felt neither mentally nor physically attracted, but also to begin this process in a place that he had never liked. The bar the shopgirl had suggested was Nottingham's only *cocktails only* bar, and what sort of man drank cocktails? Kathy, on the other hand, had always preferred a good-old-fashioned pint, and yet he was unable to ask her if she'd like to go for one ...

Eoin set his phone down, put the perfume back in its bag and stuffed the bag in the wastepaper basket. Then he picked up the miniature pencil and re-opened his diary. The box for Saturday was full up, as were all the ones for all the days that had preceded it, but Sunday, which hadn't happened yet, was free. He put the pencil between his lips, and then took it out again, and under Sunday wrote: I miss you. He paused, and then once again wrote: I miss you. And then: I miss you, I miss you, I miss you. And then: Do you miss me?

Katarzyna who is Sometimes Kasia and Sometimes Kathy but Never Katie

KATARZYNA KWIATKOWSKA SAT IN THE Broadway Cinema café-bar. On one side of her was a cup of black coffee, and on the other was Jackson's laptop, on which her application to a film school that was not in Nottingham was displayed in Arial Bold:

Your supporting statement (minimum 750 words, maximum 1,000 words) should detail your reasons for applying to the programme, previous film experience and any other information that you feel will support your application.

Before it switched to Cambria:

I have ten GCSEs (all A*–B), which I obtained from English Martyrs, and am currently studying on the Access to Media Level Three Diploma at New College, Nottingham. The nature of the course is such that students are able to gain experience in a variety of different mediums including documentary film—

And then to Times New Roman red:

Firstly, don't begin by listing your qualifications – that's what the qualifications section is for. Secondly, remember that the statement is an opportunity to talk about you, personally. For example, there's been a big gap between your leaving school and going back to college – why?

Katarzyna took a sip of black coffee, which she was teaching herself to like in the same way that she was teaching herself to like wine except that wine was easier, and considered Jackson's comments. She understood what he was saying, mainly that if she wanted to become a middle-class cosmopolitan then she needed to act like a working-class immigrant, and although on the one hand she considered this distasteful, she also really, really wanted the film school that was not in Nottingham to offer her a place – so she cracked her knuckles until they made a sound like a fourth-floor window shattering, and then began to type:

I was born in Sneinton, Nottingham, which meant that all of our neighbours were Irish or Polish, and that for the first few years of my life I thought that everyone's surname either began with an 'O' or ended in a 'ska' or a 'ski'. My parents went to great lengths to make sure that I went to a Catholic secondary school, however, which meant that I attended a secondary school in another, very different part of town ...

Then she paused, took another sip of coffee, and typed 'www. hotmail.com' into the navigation bar, and then her email and then her password, and one new, unread email from Eoin with the subject header 'Hello ...' appeared on the screen. She took another sip of coffee, clicked back to her supporting statement, and typed in the following:

I told everyone to call me Kathy because I thought that it would help me to fit in, which it probably would have done had everyone else been either Irish or old. But everyone else was middle class and young, and all the Katherines and the Kathryns and the Catherines and the Cathryns were Katies, and all of the Katies lived very different lives ...

Then she took another sip of black coffee, and clicked back onto the Hotmail tab again and stared at her new and unread message, but did not click onto it or onto Astro Alerts because Astro Alerts was futile. Instead she opened another window and typed 'www.tarotgoddess.com' into the navigation bar, and clicked on One Card Oracle. She took another sip of black coffee, and then selected the Rider Waite deck because, according to the website the Rider Waite deck was the most powerful online divination tool available, and then she clicked onto the image of the back of the Rider Waite deck that appeared.

The image of the back of the Rider Waite deck then morphed into the image of a turning Rider Waite card, which morphed into the image of a naked woman pouring jars of water into a pool beneath a moonlit sky. The words directly below the image said 'THE STAR', and below that a slightly longer text:

Success, good fortune, creativity. All is well with the world. Your highest hopes are supported by the universe. Any feelings of insecurity and un-worthiness are to be banished from your thoughts. Follow your dreams without fear or censure.

Katarzyna finished her black coffee, which she still hadn't learnt to like, clicked back to her supporting statement and typed in the following:

Last year a man from another country left me for another country and when he left it broke my heart. I decided to make a documentary about the experience, and the fiction and the horror and the death that I im-agined all around me, but also the romance and the flowers . . .

Stan who is also Stanisław who is also Stańko who is a Joke in English but a Hero in Gdańsk

STANISŁAW KWIATKOWSKI WALKED UP PAST the Cathedral, past the park and towards the cemetery, which he visited every year on the anniversary of his father's death. His father wasn't buried there of course, but back in Gdańsk, but as Gdańsk was a place from which Stanisław had always striven to maintain a distance, geographical and otherwise, he preferred to remember him here, in Nottingham, instead.

Stanisław entered the cemetery and wandered amongst the gravestones until he came to the memorial for those who had been killed in the First World War. He knew that his father had, in some ways, been one of the lucky ones in the sense that, although he had died from the injuries that he had received at the hands of the police, he had not died from them until some months later – all of which meant that, unlike those who fell and rotted in Flanders Fields, or even neighbouring Gdynia, where his older brother had, along with the other rioters, received a punishment that was even harsher, he'd been buried by his family, and on consecrated ground.

Stanisław stood in front of the war memorial and inserted his fat, pink finger into the collar of his too-tight shirt, but then took it out again because he wanted to be respectful. Then he reached inside his coat, removed a bottle of vodka, unscrewed the top and took a swig. And then he poured a little onto the ground beneath the war memorial the same way that he had seen the gypsies do because what was he himself if not a Roma or a wandering, albeit Catholic Jew?

'Solidarność,' said Stanisław, raising the bottle aloft and then watching as the vodka seeped into the earth, before then raising it higher still. 'Solidarność!'

'Well really!' said a voice behind him. 'There ought to be a law against it.'

'We'll call the police if you don't stop it,' said another.

Stanisław turned round to see two women dressed in black. One of them was clutching a bunch of chrysanthemums, and the other was waving a trowel.

'I am remembering my father,' said Stanisław, making a small bow and remembering the wet blood and the dried blood and the red and brown and black blood in the video, and the old blood from Poland that, together with the screaming and the crying were burned on both his eyes. 'And it is filling me with the emotions, but please, it is not my intention to cause you the offence.'

The woman clutching the bunch of chrysanthemums took a step forward, and then looked at the memorial, which commemorated a war that had ended forty years prior to Stanisław's birth, and all the names on which – Allsop, Brooks and so on – had a distinctly English sound.

'What the dead want most is peace and quiet,' she said eventually.

'Yes,' said her companion, her head bobbing up and down like a crow. 'That's why, in England, we say rest in peace.'

They turned their backs on him and went over to another, more recent-looking grave. The woman with the chrysanthemums began to arrange them in a vase attached to the headstone, and the one who had been waving the trowel now began to pull out the weeds on the patch of earth in front of it. Stanisław watched them for a moment, and then took another swig. He sat down on the grass which still bore the traces of last week's snow, some of which soaked into the seat of his trousers, and he pressed his hands against his eyes. His whole body began to shake with what could have been laughter or could have been crying, although even he himself could not be sure. And then, when he at last removed his hands and looked out through his watery eyes, he saw that the war memorial was no longer one stable slab of stone, but a fragmented, shimmering obelisk which confirmed that yes, the whole of the world, as he knew it, was trembling.

'Amen,' said Stanisław as the stone danced and wept in front of him, and then, 'Amen!'

He raised the vodka bottle to his lips, and as he took his final swig he heard one of the women say, 'Well if they don't even know how to look after themselves . . .'

Stanisław turned to look at her, and then contemplated the now empty vodka bottle which also trembled in an empty, glassy shimmer, and then he threw it, as hard as he could against the war memorial, where it smashed into hundreds of pieces.

'Well really!' said one of the woman who was now waving the trowel again, and in his direction, 'it just isn't decent.'

'Don't worry, I'm sure he'll get bored soon,' said the other.

Stanisław pressed his hands to his eyes again. He looked at them and then back at the war memorial, and everything trembled or twinkled through his tears until the revulsion and the anger, and then finally his liberation from them, began to roll across his alcoholic cheeks. He felt contempt for the two women, and for all who like them thrived on hate, and he wanted them to know how he felt and then feel ashamed.

'But what you expect?' shouted Stanisław, in a voice that was loud enough, he hoped, to wake the dead. 'I am Jew! Gypsy! Traitor! What in the hell do you expect?'

Meg who is also Meghu
who is also Meghana who is
also a Cloud in a Cave

MEGHANA BUDANNAVAR EXAMINED THE FOUR pink sandstone pillars framed against the rest of the pink sandstone
rock framed within the viewfinder, and pressed the button on
the top of her camera. Then she untangled the camera strap
from around her neck, turned to the Australian backpackers
beside her, and said, 'Excuse me, but would you mind taking a
picture?'

'Sure thing darl.' And one of them stepped away from the rest
of the group. 'Just let me know when you're ready.'

Meghana handed the Australian backpacker her camera, and
then positioned herself in front of the steps leading up to the
temple which was also a cave (and which was situated in the
north-west part of Karnataka, which was in the south-west part
of India, which was still several hundred miles away from her
extended family in Bangalore) and the Australian backpacker
pressed the button on the top of it.

'Thanks, that's really kind of you,' said Meghana.

'No worries darl,' said the Australian backpacker.

Meghana watched as he untangled the camera strap from
around his neck and returned to the rest of the group. Then she
turned the camera over and pressed some of the other buttons on
it until she found the 'gallery'. She scrolled through the 'gallery'
until she found the picture that she had just taken of the temple,

followed by the picture that the Australian backpacker had just taken of her outside of it.

Meghana scrutinised the picture, the majority of which consisted of the orange dress that she was wearing, and behind it the blue and cloudless sky. Only a little of the cliff into which the temple had been carved was visible, and as she contemplated the parts of herself that were orange, and the parts of the sky that were blue, she remembered that orange and blue were complementary colours, and that she must send Dave a postcard, at some point, soon . . .

Meghana pressed the button on the side of her camera that turned it off and went back over to the Australian backpackers, thinking that it was such a relief to be with them and not her extended family. Her younger cousins called her 'the little English missy' and teased her, constantly, about her accent, while her grandparents fussed over her, and stuffed her with so many sweets that she now had a little potbelly, a situation that had forced her to conclude that, despite the hot and foreign setting, their home was little better than *The Post* . . .

Meghana followed the Australian backpackers towards the first cave. She had already read about the complex in English, which meant that she already knew that UNESCO had filed it under 'Evolution of Temple Architecture' – which sounded a bit like something that Kathy, or another bona fide arty type, might have chosen as the subject of a documentary. She ran her hands across the carvings that marked the entrance, but then, as soon as she went inside, she pushed them back into her pockets, where they remained, because there was too much to see and to touch and to pretend not to touch that she daren't commit to any one thing in particular.

'Hey darl, you wanna move a little faster? We've still got three more of these buggers to get through!' shouted another Australian backpacker, or maybe the same Australian backpacker as before.

'Don't worry I'll catch you up!'

'Sure thing darl.'

233

The Australian backpackers began to file out of the cave, leaving Meghana behind them. As soon as the last one of them had departed she began to turn around, very slowly. At first she stood so that she was looking back outside where the baked red earth rose and then fell into the azure water, but then as she rotated she saw the sandstone colonnade that led to a cross-legged Vishnu. She stopped, and gazed at it for a long, long time, and then she began to walk towards it, her footsteps simultaneously scrunching and echoing across the rocky ground. All around her were sculptures of gods and goddesses with sculptures of animals and flowers and birds all around them, with sculptures of serpents and supernatural beings all around them, each of which appeared to seep into and thus embrace the other . . .

Meghana stopped again, and listened to the sound of her own breathing filling up her empty ears. A few seconds before, each footfall had marked her presence as a stranger within the temple, but now each breath seemed to whistle through her as though she herself were a part of it. She breathed in and out, feeling her ribcage expanding and deflating, and with each breath she became conscious of something that she could not have experienced in England, because she would not have been able either to describe or analyse it within the context of the university – which she now reminded herself was a European invention, and therefore not an invention that she needed. She felt privy to a new, subterranean world in which the rock and the heavens were being filtered through a giant piece of rose quartz crystal, and that she was floating through this crystal world and dancing and merging with it – and then she became conscious, above all, of love.

Dr Goldstein who is also Dave who is also David the Second King of Israel and Judah Twinned with West Bridgford and Forest Fields in Nottingham

DR DAVID GOLDSTEIN CLICKED ON the words 'log in' in the top right-hand corner of the webpage, and then entered his email and password and clicked on the words 'update blog'. Then he uploaded the file that Paul had just sent him, and then he cut and pasted a link to *forestfieldsholistic.tumblr.com* below it and said to the screen:

'I am not spiritual and I am not religious but I do enjoy finding out about other cultures on the Internet.' And the young woman from the flat downstairs and his former colleague Paul, who were standing behind him looking at the screen over his shoulder, said the same thing back to him.

David took off the kippah that he had accidently stolen from the synagogue, and looked for his nicotine gum, which he had misplaced during the ritual. He failed to find it, shut his laptop and said, 'Well thanks guys that's been an, err, massive help.' And then stood up and went over to the door.

'Yes it was certainly an um, interesting experience,' said Paul, taking David's seat.

'Yes, but you you mustn't let me take up any more of your, err, time,' said David, going to the door and holding it open. 'I'm sure that you've got lots to do.'

'Um, not really,' said Paul.

'Well, let me know if you need anything else,' said the young woman from the flat downstairs, while packing up her crystals.

'Oh yes thanks again, and, err, bye,' said David.

He continued to hold the door open as the young woman and her bags of quartz wafted through it.

'Nice, um, place you've got here,' said Paul, now also looking round.

'Thanks. It's just the right size for one person.'

David continued to hold the door open while Paul leaned back in his chair and looked round. He could see that the world outside the window above Paul's head was cold and white and covered in snow, whereas the image of Meg, despite the traces of congealed egg that now clung to the bottom of it, still shone with a marigold light; and then he realised that Paul, who was still leaning back in his chair, was looking increasingly at home . . .

'Look, I'm sorry to be rude but I'm meant to be Skyping someone in an hour or so, so I'm going to have to, err . . .' said David.

'But I thought that you might want to have a quick game of Warhammer.'

'Well normally I'd love to but, err . . .'

'Tomorrow then?'

'Well you see the thing is that I'm actually pretty, err, busy these days and, err . . .'

David allowed his lies to trail off and remained standing at the door, until Paul finally got to his feet and despondently sloped past him. Then he threw himself down onto his bed and pushed his face into his pillow, then rolled over onto his side and reached for the packet of nicotine gum, which he could now see had fallen between separate piles of rubbish on the floor. He popped out a piece and put it in his mouth, and began to chew, the medicinal taste making him wince with displeasure. He thought about how everyone who subscribed to his blog was either a conspiracy theorist or a teenage geek, and that, if he was going to be completely honest with himself, their comments lacked any kind of intellectual rigour.

He thought about his trip to the Cathedral, or more specifically, the conversation he'd had with Stan outside of it, Stan's question as to whether he had lost people in the Holocaust, and his own uncertain mumblings in reply. In truth he had lost his paternal great-grandfather, two great-aunts and some of their cousins, who were also his great-cousins something removed, none of whom either he or his father had met. He knew that he had no claims to suffering, and could therefore only imagine, from the relative comfort of his not particularly comfortable flat, what such a state of being might actually entail ... And then he thought about Meg again, who in reality had ignored his invitation to Skype and who he now decided that, for the present moment at least, he hated ...

David spat out his nicotine gum. He got up off the bed and went back over to the desk. He logged onto his email, where there were still no new or unread messages, and then he thought well fuck you bitch, paused for a moment and clicked on 'compose':

Dear Professor Woźniak,
   I am contacting you with regard to the recently advertised research position, which I believe would complement my current interests in post-modern magik and the role of ritual within a secular society. Please let me know if you would be free to discuss this further.
   Warm Regards,
      Dr Goldstein

Margaret of The Meadows Twinned with Basra and Belfast

MARGARET O'SHEA PERCHED ON THE edge of a large, overblown settee and bent her hand so that it resembled the top of a little table. She held it there for a moment or so before pulling her knuckles back until it resembled a little claw, and then she repeated each of these exercises five times. Then she took out her rosary, beginning, as always, with the Joyful Mysteries, but instead of inserting the extra prayer, as requested by the Blessed Virgin at Fatima, or even adding a quick Hail Holy Queen at the end, she whizzed straight through, put in her hearing aid, and waited.

Margaret waited for something she couldn't quite imagine but at the same time was sure would come, and as she did so she pretended to read the *Evening Post* just in case Eoin came in now. The main headline said 'More Snow Over Notts', even though there was more snow over the whole of the UK and not just this one small corner of the East Midlands, while the subheadline stated 'Woman Could Not Blink for Five Months'.

Margaret waited and listened to the sound of Eoin's footsteps, which bore down through the ceiling above her, and on top of it the clock that just wouldn't stop ticking; and as she continued to wait and to listen to both of these sounds they became jumbled up, not only with each other but also with all of the patterns and the puppies and the gilt-edged plates until she could hardly bear it anymore because surely, *surely* there must be other, more important things than snow or not blinking, and that surely, *surely* one of them must be about to break the spell and happen to her now?

Margaret stood up, shuffled slowly up the stairs to what was once again Eoin's room, and then stood outside the door and waited. His footsteps had stopped, and in their place a faint, scratchy sound that could have been a chair being pulled back, or a pen nib against a piece of paper, or perhaps some other thing she hadn't thought of yet even though she had racked and racked her brain in an attempt to cover every possibility; but she kept on waiting and listening, and then after a minute or so she raised her voice and said, 'Can I come in?'

The scratching stopped and then: 'I'm just in the middle of something Nana, but I'll be down again soon I promise.'

'Only I was going to make a cup of tea?'

'Honestly Nana I'm fine.'

'Well if you're sure . . .?'

Margaret stood and waited outside the door even though she now couldn't hear any sounds at all. She wondered if Eoin was thinking about her or his mother, whose picture he had taken to carrying with him, or Kathy, whom Albertina claimed to have seen outside New College talking to an Indian woman; and then she shuffled back downstairs and went into the kitchen.

She was aware that her knees were aching less than usual and that her hand was able to grasp things better than usual and that her hearing aid, which still fizzed and crackled at all the wrong moments, was nevertheless bothering her slightly less than usual too; and then she wondered what on earth a supposedly nice, good Catholic girl like Kathy was doing talking to Muslims instead of being here with her and Eoin now?

Margaret shook her head and put the kettle on just as the clock struck twelve and then she began to say The Angelus simply because she always said The Angelus at that time of day. As soon as the water had boiled she poured it into the teapot, and as soon as the tea had brewed she poured it into her teacup – only she had forgotten about the broken spout, which made the water spurt unevenly all over her already damaged hand ...

'Be it done unto me according to Your Word,' said Margaret, but did not go any further with her prayer.

Instead she picked up the kettle again, and poured the rest of its contents over the back of her other, weaker hand, while screwing up her eyes, until the whole of her body ceased to be a body and was just a vessel for the pain. Her eyelids flickered. Her broken hand twitched. And then she pressed her lips together so that what mustn't get out stayed in.

Acknowledgements

Thank you to Hannah Westland, without whose support, encouragement and intelligent sensitivity this novel might not exist. Thank you also to the very charming Leonora Craig Cohen, Patrick Taylor, Anna-Marie Fitzgerald and all the other brilliant people at Serpent's Tail. Likewise, thank you to my lovely agent Nicola Barr.

Thank you to Andreas Korte for being a great boyfriend and always having faith in my abilities.

Thank you to Tom Cowdrey for providing feedback on an early draft, and pointing out, quite rightly, that no one ever eats homemade custard creams.

Thank you to Meg and Vijayendra Bisineer for their advice on all things Lingayat; Katie Horwich and Caterina Lewis for their insights on being both secular and Jewish; Katy Soar for explaining just what you can and cannot get away with in a Geography Department; Omar Fazal and Tomasz John for sharing their experiences of communist Poland; and Jane Fawcett for accompanying me on my visits to the Hindu temple, and lending me the phrase 'snakes with tits'.

Thank you to Elinor Cooper, Samantha Talbot and Mimei Thompson for their friendship in London, and to James Harding and Phoebe Blatton for their friendship in Berlin, as well as, in the latter case, introducing me to golonka and explaining all the ways her father's name can be abbreviated.

Last but not least thank you to Tessa Baird and Jane Cheadle who have been my unofficial proof-readers, editors and life-coaches since forever and to whom, with much love, this book is dedicated.